THE KID COMES BACK

BOOKS BY

JOHN R. TUNIS

Published by William Morrow & Company
HIS ENEMY, HIS FRIEND 1967
SILENCE OVER DUNKERQUE 1962
SCHOOLBOY JOHNSON 1958
BUDDY AND THE OLD PRO 1955
GO, TEAM, GO! 1954
YOUNG RAZZLE 1949
HIGHPOCKETS 1948
THE KID COMES BACK 1946

Published by Harcourt, Brace & Company
A CITY FOR LINCOLN 1945
ROOKIE OF THE YEAR 1944
YEA! WILDCATS! 1944
KEYSTONE KIDS 1943
ALL-AMERICAN 1942
WORLD SERIES 1941
CHAMPION'S CHOICE 1940
THE KID FROM TOMKINSVILLE 1940
THE DUKE DECIDES 1939
IRON DUKE 1938

THE KID
COMES BACK

J O H N   R .   T U N I S

WILLIAM MORROW & CO., INC.
NEW YORK

PUBLISHER'S NOTE: On baseball teams before
1950, unlike those of today, it was not unusual for
the team's manager to also play one of the posi-
tions in the field. In this book, Spike Russell is
both the Dodgers' manager and its shortstop.

THE KID COMES BACK

CHAPTER

1

USUALLY as they climbed into the waiting truck outside the Operations Tent, Roy thought, How romantic all this would be if only I weren't going through it myself. Somehow that night it wasn't even abstractly romantic. There was no romance in it, none whatever.

Well, he thought, we didn't have any too good reports on this one, this job of taking supplies to the Underground in Occupied France. That was plain enough in the Operations Tent when the intelligence officer showed us the pictures. We all knew it, every one of us felt it. These night flights are invariably hot missions. And the fact is, Roy realized, this thing is beginning to get me down.

The truck jolted and bumped down the road out to the field, and across to their waiting plane. They clambered down, yanking at their flak vests and chutes, and stood round, waiting. The worst ten minutes of all, the wait before they could take off— like the last minutes before a team takes the field in a Rose Bowl game, or the final contest in a World Series. The same craving for action, the same desire to do something, to release twitching muscles and tight lips. There was no emotion, no joking, no moving picture stuff. Just four extremely tired men waiting to do the unpleasant job they had been doing as far back as they could recall, as far as time stretched.

Scotty wandered round and round the little group blowing half-audible runs and trills on his harmonica. Earl sat on his chute, checking his compass. Jim leaned over to load his automatic. The others carried 45's; but Roy, the tail gunner, had little room to move about in, so he wore a long-handled knife which he stuffed in his belt. For the same reason he had a chest-type parachute, with the harness attached to his body, and the chute on the floor under his seat when in flight.

Roy watched the mechanics readying the plane, as he had done dozens of times before. There were half a dozen of them, on top, underneath, inside, around the gas truck, all chattering in the quiet night air; all oblivious to the task awaiting the ship and the crew who flew her. Snatches of their conversation came to him.

"My wife writes, now she says eggs are sixty cents a dozen. Things keep on this-a-way, she says . . ."

"Got a letter from home this morning, and wha'd'ya think the little tyke wants to know? Wants to know all about this Brooklyn boy in the squadron, this here now Roy Tucker."

Roy turned away. He had heard them like that, listened to the grease monkeys, watched them do the same things dozens of times before. Somehow that night they bothered him. All at once he wanted to yell at them as loud as he could. Hey, look, you guys; you up there in the turret, and you, Bud, out on the wing, and you, fella, you gassing her up, and you two in the truck. Look, we're taking this ship up tonight, and maybe we won't come back. Maybe we'll ditch or crash somewhere in France or something. And we've got people at home, same as you have.

Aw, what's the use? They wouldn't understand what's biting me. He turned away. Suddenly Earl rose and began climbing aboard. Jim was going up after him. O.K., here goes. But those mechanics, they're sure something, those guys.

Jim, the pilot, immediately started checking his gauges, while Roy climbed into his place in the rear of the plane and adjusted the phones over his head. "Let's have another time check, boys; let's have one more to make sure," said Jim. "In twelve seconds it'll be ten minutes to ten. Nine seconds . . . eight . . . seven . . . six . . . five . . . four . . . three . . . O.K.! That's it."

Once again his voice came to them. "Pilot to tail gunner. Do you receive?"

Roy's tone was cracked and queer as he heard himself reply. This is no good, no good at all, he thought. I'm getting jittery. "Tail gunner to pilot. Receiving you loud and clear." Now the mechanics were scattering. They'll go back to their tents and sleep in bed tonight, while we'll be somewhere in France trying to find the headquarters of the *Maquis,* a pinpoint on a map.

At last the engines roared, one after the other. The plane bounced down the runway, and stopped for the final check. Then the ground rushed away underneath, there was the beautiful free movement as the ship caught the air and left the earth below,

and Jim, climbing on course, swung over the airfield.
Once they were airborne Roy noticed, as he invariably did, how little of their actual operations on
the ground showed from above. The squadron had
learned something since their debarkation at Algiers
eighteen months before.

Now Casamozza vanished, and the field disappeared. Then underneath lay Bastia, a cluster of
white, familiar houses with red roofs grouped about
the tiny harbor, sharp and distinct in the moonlight.
As they climbed, the remainder of the island with
its mountain peaks came into his vision. He bent
over to load his guns. When he lifted his head again,
Corsica was vanishing fast astern. They were over
the Tuscan sea, and slowly swinging round to point
for France.

For perhaps two hours they were above water,
then across the French coastline and over the moon-
lit countryside before Roy became worried. It was
Jim's voice, stiff and tight, that confirmed suspicions
which had been deepening for some minutes. Over
the intercom came those familiar tones.

"Pancake Z. Pancake Z. This is Fried Spratt calling Pancake Z. Fried Spratt calling Pancake Z."

They waited, all four of them: the pilot up front,

and Scotty, the turret gunner, and Earl, the bombardier in the waist, and Roy himself in the tail. They waited for nothing because nothing happened. There was no reply from their base on Corsica. Only the usual hum of the intercom.

Boy, are we lost? It couldn't be we're lost, thought Roy. Jim'll make it somehow; he always has. He got us through on that run over Anzio and Highway 7; on that nasty job we had at the Fiat works in Turin, when we lost Elmer at Leghorn, and the time the Messerschmitt jumped us over the Mediterranean. He'll do it this time, too; he's a good chauffeur, Jim is.

"Pancake Z. Pancake Z. This is Fried Spratt calling Pancake Z."

There it was again. No use talking, we're lost this time. Yep, no fooling, we're lost. Say, isn't that something! Fifty-six missions over Italy and France, then this. We're really lost.

It was chilly, so Roy in the tail gunner's seat wore coveralls and a sweater. Suddenly he felt sweat across his forehead. Why, this is terrible, this is awful, this feeling of fear. The fact is, I'm afraid.

We're lost now; no mistake, either.

CHAPTER
2

ONCE more they waited, listening, all of them, Scotty in the turret, and Earl in the middle, and Roy squeezed into the tail of the plane. They listened like shipwrecked men, for that was what they were, shipwrecked in the skies, adrift, uncertain. Far below, that misty streak was the Rhone or the valley of the Durance or even the valley of the Dordogne, which they had been supposed to follow. They might be right after all.

Still no response from the base.

Suddenly the answer came, loud and strong, wonderfully reassuring. All at once, the way it invariably happened, for no reason at all the base came through. The whole ship seemed to lighten at the sound of the voice on the other end.

"Hello, Fried Spratt. Hello, Fried Spratt. Give me

a long signal. Hello, Fried Spratt, this is Pancake Z calling. Give me a signal."

The exultant tones in Jim's voice penetrated every heart as he began to count in firm, even tones. "One . . . two . . . three . . . four . . . five . . . six . . . seven . . . eight . . . nine . . . ten . . . over, Pancake Z."

They listened to the answer. And the voice of Jim again, asking for a bearing.

"Fried Spratt to Pancake Z. Fried Spratt calling Pancake Z. Can you give me a bearing now?"

Instantly, too quickly almost, the voice responded. "Pancake Z to Fried Spratt. Pancake Z calling Fried Spratt. Take up a heading of 220 degrees south, and come in at 5,000. Take a heading of 220 degrees south, and come in at 5,000."

"Fried Spratt to Pancake Z. Fried Spratt calling Pancake Z. O.K., Pancake Z, willco. Willco."

He switched off. Now there was silence save for the steady roar of the two Wright engines humming through the night. This boy Jim, he's good. I'm just getting jittery; I've had about enough, that's the trouble with me.

They had gone on for several seconds before Roy spoke up from his cubbyhole.

[8]

"Hey there, Jim! D'ja notice anything strange about that one?"

"No. Why?" The pilot, instantly suspicious, replied immediately.

"I dunno. Just the way the guy talked, the way he said the word 'degrees.' He called it 'degwees,' d'ja notice?"

"I sure noticed it. Sounded kinda funny to me," Scotty came in.

"Now you mention it, believe I did, too." Earl's voice was excited.

"Well, we'd better go in at ten thousand and see what happens," the pilot said.

The plane rose slowly into the darkness. Far below an occasional light in a farm or cottage showed where the windows had been insufficiently covered, and there were dim outlines of blacked-out towns along the way. They went on for some minutes, watching carefully, all of them.

Yet although they were watching and waiting, everyone half expecting it, when it came they were astonished. Without warning, the darkness below them was suddenly filled with the bright streaks of flak. The fireworks appeared in the night air, died away, and flared up again. Every flak gun in the occupied countries seemed to be spraying the heavens, while they sailed along serenely five thousand feet above the fracas.

"Let's get out of here," said Scotty. The place was far too unhealthy, because those near-by clouds could easily shelter enemy planes, waiting just for them. Jim gave her the gun, and soon they were leaving the fireworks far behind.

Trying later on to remember exactly what happened, Roy had trouble recalling just how long it took Jim to get them back on their course. Too much took place and in far too short a space of time for anyone to have a clear picture of the events that followed. Nor could Roy remember which one of the crew it was who actually picked out the tiny landing field in the misty valley below. Was it Scotty's voice who broke in? Or Earl's?

"Say! What's that?"

"What? Where?"

"Those lights. See there!"

"Lights? What lights? I don't see any lights."

"Over there. About sixty degrees, beyond that town there. See the town?"

"I see the town, but I don't see any lights."

"Hey, I do, I do."

[10]

"Oh, sure, I do now. I didn't at first, but I see 'em now all right."

"Me, too."

The whole crew was watching now with attention. Roy twisted in his seat to get a glimpse of those lights which could mean their objective at last or nothing more than an isolated farmhouse with windows uncovered. Also, he reflected, it could be Germans signaling from below in the hopes of trapping them. Things like that had been known to happen before.

Certainly, however, that town could be the one, that could be Bergerac, and that twisting stretch of silver could be the river Dordogne. It looked exactly like the setup that had been described to them.

Then somebody was flashing a signal from below. Obviously it was a signal, whether to them or someone else. Two green lights and a red; two green lights and a red.

"There they go. That's us, Jim!"

"Looks like it. But we'll just take things easy. Let's be sure this time. We got ourselves out of one tight spot tonight; let's not walk head first into another. Let's make it sure."

"That's right. Give 'em the signal, Jim."

The pilot turned a switch which lit up a signal lamp on the plane, and immediately a green light winked three times from below. Plain to see this was no flak-protected and well-organized German airdrome, but a small, secret landing field of the French Underground. As far as they could tell from above, the field was isolated enough to be some distance from any indiscreet neighbors.

Jim descended lower and lower, preparatory to landing. They waited. Finally he spoke.

"Landing gear's stuck."

Landing gear stuck! Hang it all, if it isn't one thing it's another, this trip. First we're plain lost. Then we get ourselves out of a slick Jerry trap. Next the landing gear has to stick. Fifty-six missions over Europe and then this.

CHAPTER

3

ONCE again they rose in the night. Jim went to four thousand and tried to operate the hand pump to pump hydraulic pressure into the lines. Then he pulled the manual release on the floor which should have released the safety latch and dropped the wheels out of the nacelles. Nothing happened. Mechanical failure; or perhaps a stray bit of flak had broken the cables. Anyway the wheels did not budge. Jim tried every possible maneuver to shake them free. He fluttered the ship from side to side, dropped in a terrific dive, and then pulled them suddenly out of it. Next he wrenched them up and down until their stomachs were sore. The landing gear was stuck and no mistake.

Even before the orders came through from Jim, Roy realized what it meant—a belly landing. He unhitched himself from his guns, felt for the knife at his side and the compass in his pocket. At his feet was his escape kit. It contained benzedrine, caramels, chewing gum, a small map, and forty dollars in French bills.

Here's one time it will be useful, too!

What had he been told? He tried to recall the instructions given at briefing from time to time; told until it all became an old story one heard but hardly listened to. With all his heart he wished he had paid more attention. What was it now? Lie low for twenty-four hours. If you can hide for twenty-four hours, the Germans usually stop searching the locality, and likely enough you'll be all right. Avoid all cities. Contact only poor people—farmers and workmen. Well, we'll most probably do that, judging by this countryside below.

They were lower now, lower still. After circling the field once more, Jim approached from the northern end of the small runway. Gently, under his trained hands, the ship was descending into the blackness.

Roy scrambled hastily out of the turret and caught a glimpse of Earl's tense and anxious face. Earl was stowing the lower gun, which he finally secured in its place. Then he slammed the bottom hatch door. In moments such as these one didn't really think, one acted automatically; one was a robot following directions heard dozens of times on how to prepare for a belly landing. Well, this is it. We're for it now.

Roy grabbed his flak helmet from the floor of the ship and jammed it on, signaling to Earl to do the same thing. This was protection against having one's head cracked open. Roy knew perfectly well that when the ship landed, there was no telling what they might be smashed against or where.

Next he snatched his parachute pack from the side of the plane, placed it on the floor, and lay down, his head resting on the chute as protection. Earl crawled across and placed himself on the floor between Roy's legs, with his hands bracing the back of his head against the gunner's stomach. Roy, in turn, braced his feet against the back of the turret to prevent himself from being thrown forward when the ship actually struck.

Now they were ready. Nothing to do but wait, the hardest moments of all. They lay there listening to the roar of the engines change gradually to a hum as Jim eased up on the throttles. Make it good, boy,

make it good. Seconds were years for the two figures locked together in the rear of the plane, unable to help, nervously waiting. There was a strong
westerly wind, and the pilot was giving the ship
lots of rudder to keep it on an even keel. They were
coming down now. Roy could smell trees and the
sweet dampness of earth.

The plane descended, bit by bit, searching for
the ground. It continued to drop; still no contact.
Then there was a sudden, raucous grinding, which
turned into a deafening roar. Next a spine-cracking
jolt as the ship struck and plowed through the
improvised landing field, sliding along on its belly,
tearing up the ground with a terrific noise. With the
jolt, everything went out from under Roy. A hundred, a thousand bands were playing, all together.
He started falling into a bottomless abyss, down,
down, away from the groaning engines and the
screaming ship. He fell with no consciousness of a
fall. He fell until there was silence all around.

When he came to, he was lying on the ground,
pain shooting up and down his back, his head dizzy.
For some moments he lay still, unable to move. Finally he tried to rise, and as he did so was violently
sick, retching on the ground in agony. He sank back

exhausted, conscious only of the intense pain in his back. Voices came from a long way off, loud, excited, strange tones. Suddenly he was surrounded in the darkness by a crowd of yelling, gesticulating foreigners. They helped him to his feet and held him up, talking continually. Their patois was so much Chinese as far as he was concerned. All he knew, all he felt, all his world was that pain in his back.

Someone handed him a flask. It was wine, strong and sour, but he drank eagerly and handed it back. Then with an arm over the shoulder of each man beside him, he hobbled along.

4

THE room was large and low. At one end was a zinc bar. Overhead, from huge black beams, hung two smoking oil lamps, and the place was thick with the smoke from dozens of pipes. There were tables, and seated at the tables, playing cards, was the worst-looking gang of bandits Roy had ever seen. The bandits rose together and surrounded the crew of Fried Spratt with friendly exclamations of interest and delight. At least they were not hostile bandits. Chairs were shoved out for the four Americans. A red wine was hastily poured from a bottle into thick glasses and handed to each of them. Over everything were the noise and the shouting and the laughter of thirty or forty men all talking together at the same time. Only a machine gun here and there at someone's elbow showed that this was a nation at war.

"Tough-looking hombres, hey?" Earl, across the table, raised his eyebrows.

"Boy, you said it!" replied Roy.

Now the bandits were surrounding them, drinking toasts, clinking glasses, patting each one on the shoulder, shaking their hands, examining their clothing, admiring their 45's with cries of interest.

Roy looked at them closely, like people from the moon. A few hours ago we ate dinner in the mess at Casamozza; here we are in the heart of France, in occupied territory, with Germans all around and these roughnecks our only hope of escape.

"Sure glad they're on our side."

"Me, too," said Earl soberly.

Roy sipped the wine which was red, thick and extremely sour, regarding the circle with somewhat the same curiosity as that with which they regarded him. The bandits wore all sorts of strange costumes, none alike. Some had on furry coats, quite evidently made by the wearer from the skins of trapped animals; others, business suits, torn and shabby, with dirty shirts open at the neck and much the worse for continued wear; or odd bits of foreign uniforms,

[19]

here a green German blouse, there a pair of khaki breeches, or English shorts topped by a blue French army jacket. Some wore stiff leather puttees round their legs; a few had wrapped strips of cloth between their shoe tops and their knees. Their footwear was even more astonishing; high boots that laced up the calf, sneakers, queer slippers of cloth with rope soles. A few even had on shoes made of abandoned tires, fastened together with pieces of string, that they had obviously fashioned themselves. Their appearance as a group was worse because most of them had not seen a razor recently—if at all. Every imaginable sort of beard, from a soft, silky down to a long, stiffish gray one, was visible.

A tough-looking bunch of hombres, as Earl remarked. Well, we don't look any too handsome ourselves right now. Roy glanced at Earl's forehead bandaged with a dingy white handkerchief, at Jim's torn uniform, at his own soiled coveralls, the trousers cut above the knee where they had scraped on some piece of jagged metal when he was thrown from the plane. They were all hot, tired, and dirty.

"How's the back, kid?" Jim stood over him.

"It's not too good, Jim. That farm cart sure gave it a shaking up. Guess I'll be O.K. though." He shifted a little in his chair, and the spasm of pain shot up his hip once more, just as it had all through the journey from the airfield where they had crashed.

"There's a doc coming. He'll look at you, and at that head of yours, Earl, too."

Then the French leader, the man who had given the orders to destroy their plane, came pushing through the mob around them and spoke to Jim. His tones were those of an officer used to being obeyed, although he wore civilian clothes, with a dingy muffler around his neck and a cloth cap on his head. Of the four Americans, only the pilot could talk French, and it wasn't easy for him. Yet somehow Jim and the French leader conversed, understanding each other a little, misunderstanding each other more, explaining, talking slowly, using sign language.

Roy glanced up. A small, thin, black-haired chap was watching Earl light a cigarette. The man had a machine gun crooked in his arm. Earl lighted his cigarette naturally and casually; but there was a strange intentness and fixity in the Frenchman's gaze. He glared at the full package Earl pulled from his pocket, followed the lighted match as it rose to the bombardier's mouth, watched the quick way Earl blew out the smoke. Roy seldom smoked himself, but he had a package of cigarettes in his escape kit. He opened it, took out the package, and extended it to the little black-haired man.

"Me? You give me?" He stood fixed, staring at the package in Roy's outstretched hand. Suddenly he reached across the table and grabbed it. He leaned over. "For you . . . perhaps . . . is nawtheeng, the cigarette. For me, is everytheeng. Fifteen years I work with American company in Paris; smoke American cigarette. Dan, tree, four year . . . no more American cigarette. Wan year, two year . . . no cigarette . . . none." He waved his hands. The circle of bandits listened with approval; they did not understand his words, but they knew what he was saying. Their tired eyes held the same rapture as his.

Roy watched. Now what? Will he keep them himself? Or, if cigarettes are as scarce as all that, will he pass them round? Would I pass them round if I loved smoking and hadn't seen a cigarette for two years? What will he do? This is the Underground; the famous French Underground they've told us about so many times in briefing, that we've discussed in the mess in Africa and Corsica and Italy, heard stories and yarns about from escaped pilots and others. They're wonderful; they're terrible; they're patriots; they're communists; they're generous and noble and cutthroats and murderers. Now let's see what happens.

In the smoky light of the ancient inn, the circle round the table watched also, fascinated, while the thin black-haired man with the red-rimmed eyes opened the package of cigarettes, smelled them with a long breath which brought a smile to his weary face, held them up, took one out and twisted it round slowly in his fingers.

Then he placed the cigarette gently behind his right ear, and handed the package to the next man. He took one, smelled it, and passed the package along. It went round the circle; each man with courtesy and without grabbing took a cigarette from the package, fondled it, and held it with reverent fingers. Finally it was empty. The last man took the empty package, poured the crumbs out carefully, fished a torn piece of toilet paper from his pocket, and with great care rolled a small end for himself.

Roy looked over at Earl; Earl was looking at him. "Gee," said the bombardier. "Gee!"

CHAPTER

5

THEY watched the little fellow smoke. Never before had they seen anyone smoke like that. Not as Earl or Scotty or the chaps in the mess at the base smoked, but slowly, reverently, tasting the cigarette, rolling it round in his mouth with those bony fingers, holding in the smoke, then blowing it out and smelling it at the same time, making the whole procedure last as long as possible. They were fascinated. Dimly they began to realize they were in another world, a world where things were upside down. When Earl carelessly stubbed out his butt, there was a moment's quick silence in the chatter of the group standing above them round the table. Then three bandits leaned over and reached for the butt simultaneously.

The small black-haired man, who never put down

his machine gun, began to talk. He spoke perhaps one word of English to four or five of French, thus making himself almost unintelligible. Roy was unable to understand what he said.

"Wish I'd known! I had a year of French in school and never once cracked a book. Wish I'd known back home there that it might help save my life some day."

"Same here, Roy. I had two years in high school. I can't remember a word now. What's the little geezer saying?"

"Darned if I know." There they were, the four of them; and all except Jim, who had studied French at college, were unable to understand more than a few words. Dimly Roy began to appreciate something of the meaning of that word he had used so often and heard used so often, usually without ever thinking of its real meaning. Suddenly he realized that the thing called education was not, as he had once imagined, merely a lot of useless exercises to keep youngsters confined in Jefferson High from eight-thirty to three. It meant living things, tools that were to be used later on in life. If you didn't have them, well, it was too bad for you, that's all.

Roy recalled how he spent his time in French,

which came the hour before school closed for the day. He could see the sky outside, and the trees, and could remember sitting there looking at the clouds through the open window in spring, wondering whether the rain would hold off long enough so they could play the ballgame that afternoon.

"Hey, Roy, look! Get a load of that. It's a dame, it's a girl over there. The one with the gun." Scotty, ever one with an eye to feminine society, pointed across the room. Sure enough, it was a girl, a dark, rather good-looking girl. She wore a beret, ski pants, an old khaki army blouse, and a revolver on a belt round her waist. Scotty rose and pushed back his chair.

"Say, hey there, Jim!" Earl called over to the pilot who was at a table conferring with the French leader and paid no attention. His forehead was wrinkled, he was listening hard, trying to understand the Frenchman, who was speaking slowly. It was plainly something of importance. One could see Jim's French was none too good, either.

Meanwhile the little chap with the machine gun, standing at their table, was talking.

"What's he saying? D'you get it, Roy?"

"Sure I get that, it's his name. Of course, it's his name."

"Me, Marcel . . . Marcel, me. You?"

"Me? I'm Earl."

"Earl. O.K., Earl, O.K." He extended his hand. "You? Please?"

"I'm Roy, Roy Tucker." He grasped the Frenchman's hand. It was nothing but a piece of bone.

"O.K., Roy, O.K." Apparently the term "O.K." was an important part of his knowledge of English.

"Long time no speak Eengleesh. Me, Marcel. He, Pierre." He pointed across to the table where Jim sat with their leader. "He, chief. Twanty tousand franc . . ." Then he pulled his forefinger across his neck in an expressive and curious gesture.

"I getcha. That's the guy who heads up this crowd. And the Germans have a reward for him; twenty thousand francs if he's caught." The two Americans glanced over with respect. The man sure had a tough-looking chin.

Meanwhile, the little fellow beside them, the machine gun still under one arm, had smoked the cigarette until it was almost impossible to hold. He put it out, and took the few remaining crumbs, emptying them into a small sack of tobacco which he extracted from his pocket. Then he began talking. The two Americans tried hard to understand him, while the circle of bandits above leaned over each other's shoulders to listen, wild-looking in the dim light from the kerosene lamps hanging from the beams overhead. In one corner, Scotty was fingering the revolver of the slender girl in ski pants, holding out his own 45. Quite evidently making time with her, too.

Marcel continued to talk. He was thin and pale, hardly able, one would have said, to carry a machine gun any distance; but he never relaxed his grip on it. His words were far too difficult for them to understand. They often sounded like the same thing. "Vestern," he kept saying. Over and over again he repeated himself, waiting for a signal of recognition on their faces. "Vestern . . . vestern . . . vestern . . . *compagnie* vestern."

It was Roy who understood. "Hey there, I getcha, Marcel. You're trying to say 'Western Union.'"

"*Oui . . . oui . . . oui. Compagnie Vestern,* I work there; learn Eengleesh in Paris."

"Why, sure, I know. I usta carry messages for them back home in Tomkinsville when I was a kid.

Me . . . bicycle . . . messages." He spoke slowly and distinctly. "Get it? Compree?"

"O.K. O.K." Marcel's face lit up. He was in ecstasies of delight that at last they understood he had worked for an American corporation. The bandits standing round the table patted him on the back, admiring his linguistic abilities.

"How'd you happen to get into this game, Marcel? You . . . Resistance. How come?"

"Ah!" A somber look came over his face. "Two, tree year. Me, Jew."

"Oh. I see." There was silence. "Hey, Roy, ask him are there women in the Underground, too." But Marcel did not need to be asked—he got the question.

"Many women, oh, yes. Oh, many. Women O.K. in France. Woman making wan hundred kilometers on bicyclette. This woman . . . here, this woman."

"Say! Get it? That kid talking to Scotty rides a hundred kilometers on a bike, toting that gun. How much is a hundred kilometers? Let's see, times five . . . divided by eight . . . that's nearly sixty miles. Boy!"

Then the door opened. A cold draught made the lamps flare up violently, and a gust of rain came into the room. A figure in a long cape entered. He carried a black bag underneath his cape. Instantly a dozen voices shouted at him:

"Docteur. Le docteur. Voila le docteur. Ah, docteur."

He shut the door, brushed off the rain from his shoulders, stamped his wet feet, shook hands with the chief and half a dozen others, and slung aside the cape which came down to his toes. He was a little man with eyeglasses and a goatee beard. He wore a stiff, celluloid collar. The effect was to make him rather ridiculous. But Marcel was impressed. Evidently the doctor was something in the Underground.

"Good. Ver' good docteur. He come twenty kilometers by bicyclette."

Twenty kilometers! Holy smoke; how far is that? Twelve miles! Gee, that's something! Twelve miles on a stinking rainy night like this by bike is something, all right. He looks kinda funny, but he must be a right guy to turn out for us on a night of this sort.

They watched as he came over, shook hands with them all, and then went to work on Earl immediately. He was thin and pale like the rest, but his fingers betrayed his skill, and he worked with competency and dispatch. There was a gash over the bombardier's right eye, and a swollen lump on his forehead. The doctor said little; he was the only non-talkative Frenchman they had met. With care and attention he looked the wound over in the light of a smoky lamp held for him by one of the bandits, and then said something with a tone of approval. Reaching into his bag, he produced a tiny bottle of iodine which he swabbed into the wound, making Earl wince. After that he pasted a strip of plaster over it, and applied some salve to the bump above it. Next he took up the dirty bandage, refolded it and, to the horror of the watching Americans, bound up the wound with it again.

He saw their glances and understood. His shoulders went up, his head tossed to one side, and he spoke. They got his meaning although the words were entirely foreign to them. He was saying that there were no bandages, no cloth left in all France.

Then the doctor motioned to Roy to climb upon the table. As he rose in his chair, that sudden shooting pain came up his hip once more. Stiffly he removed his muddy coveralls, and aided by the doctor climbed upon the table, lying face down. The doctor, without ceremony, yanked off his trousers, thrust his shirt up around his neck, and began running thin, cold fingers down his spine. At last he said something in rapid, staccato French to Jim, who now stood beside Roy.

"He wants you to tell him when it hurts you, Roy."

"I'll holler all right. It sure hurt me to stand up just now."

Those icy fingertips ranged up and down his back. Along his right hip, his right leg, his right calf, feeling gently at first, then pressing into the flesh, without result. Next the doctor went up the left side of his back, and so down the left hip.

"Ouch! Ouch! That hurts, plenty."

The fingers continued their probing, though more gently. The doctor exclaimed, "Ah . . . ah . . . ah!"

Down the thigh to the left leg, to the left calf. His calf was strangely sore, yet far less painful than his hip. Again the clammy fingers felt round his thigh, gently at first, then pressing in.

"Oh! There, that's it . . . there!"

This continued for some minutes. Finally he was finished. Roy sat on the edge of the table and yanked clumsily at his trousers, discovering that he was quite unable to bend over.

Meanwhile Jim, the chief, and the doctor were in a huddle at the far end of the room. Marcel, his machine gun under his arm, continued to talk or try to talk in English. Earl spoke up.

"That's a German gun. Hey, let's have a look." But the Frenchman pulled away; no one was getting that gun for a second. "Bet the guy sleeps with it," said Earl. At last Jim rejoined them.

"Now, fellas, here's the way things are. Scotty, leave that dame, will ya? C'mon over here." Scotty was still in the far corner with the girl in ski pants; he returned to their table with reluctance. "Snap into it, Scotty; this is serious. Now we're in the Dordogne, fellas, about twenty-six miles from the town of Bergerac. You were right, Earl, that *was* Bergerac we passed over. It's about fifty to sixty miles from here to Bordeaux, as I get it, and something around two hundred and fifty to three hundred miles to the Spanish border. Staying here is dangerous for both us and these boys. It's dangerous to stay and dangerous to leave, but we must try. The Resistance has it all planned out, and they've got lots of our men out before, so no reason at all why we shouldn't make it if we do what they tell us. First, we must split up."

"How's that? Split up Fried Spratt?"

"Nuts to that! We've been together, three of us have, since the States, since that first winter in North Africa, since we hit Algiers."

"Why, we can't split up! We can't separate!" They protested, all of them. You couldn't do that to Fried Spratt.

"We must, boys. It's no fun, but remember what they always told us—the Resistance knows their stuff, and we were to do whatever they said and take whatever orders were given by their leaders. We're in their hands from now on out. Here's how we'll work it. Scotty and Earl go dead south and are guided across the Pyrenees."

"Gee, Jim, you mean we walk over those mountains?"

"No, you dope, they send a Rolls-Royce for you. Where do you think you are, Scotty, in the U. S.? Or maybe you'd rather end up in a prison camp in Germany. Roy and I go southeast to the coast, where they'll probably put us on a sub or a fishing smack for Portugal. It's more dangerous, but Roy isn't able to walk much and we can get there by train. Earl's head will be all right in two-three days. Roy, the doc isn't so sure about your trouble. He thinks it might be nothing more than a severe muscle sprain that will clear up, but he's afraid it's more likely the jouncing-up displaced something in your back, something that's pressing on your sciatic nerve."

"Is that it? Whatever it is, it's sure raising Cain when I start moving round."

"He thinks most probably that's it. He can't tell for sure without an X ray. There's no chance of that out here. Anyhow, he says for the present you shouldn't exercise or even walk more than necessary; you must rest as much as possible. That's why you and I go by train. With the main lines guarded by Germans and the stations watched, it's a chance, but we hafta take it. We couldn't possibly make the Pyrenees."

"You mean *I* couldn't. You could, Jim. You shove off with Earl and Scotty."

"Nope, two and two is the order; makes it easier for these folks. Now, to escape we need three things —civilian clothes, identity cards, and a Frenchman to accompany us. They'll furnish the clothes and get us the identity cards."

"How?"

[35]

"How do I know, Scotty? You and Earl go with that chap in the blue beret there; his name is Robert."

"O.K. What's his last name?"

"Listen, dope, in the Underground you don't ask a guy his last name. You only know his tagline. That's in case you get caught, see?"

"How about that dame with the revolver? She looks like a first-class guide."

"Keep your eye on the ball for once, will ya, Scotty? She stays. You go. You go with the guy they pick out for you. Roy, you and I go with Marcel."

A voice interrupted him. It was an English voice, an extremely English voice.

"This is . . . the overseas transcription of the British Broadcasting Company, calling all Occupied France." Then followed a few sentences in French.

"Gee," said Scotty, "it's London! The B.B.C."

"Sssh." A dozen voices spoke up, twenty men turned to glare at their table. This was important.

"*Ici Londres,*" continued another voice. "*Veuillez écouter d'abord quelques messages personnels.*"

"What's he say?" whispered Earl.

"He's asking them first to listen to some personal

messages to France. Then most likely he'll give them the news."

"I getcha. A commentator," said Scotty.

"Sssh," went up the warning round the room.

The French voice kept on speaking. The roomful of bandits sat silently, their hands cupped over their ears, for the radio was turned well down. The girl in ski pants with the revolver strapped to her waist was perched on the end of a table with a notebook and pencil in her hands. She was a stenographer in civilian life; that was plain by the professional manner in which she wrote down the messages as they were spoken. There was a pause between each one. Each was repeated twice.

Jim translated in a whisper what he understood. "The station master has a red flag. Nope . . . I didn't catch that one. He wears a blue shirt . . . what's that? Oh, yes, the soup is now served, he says." Then there was a longish pause. A silence of almost thirty seconds. The voice continued:

"Les monarques sont arrivés à la mariage."

Instantly a shout rose over the smoky room. The entire crowd turned to the crew of Fried Spratt, yelling.

"Say! What d'you think of that! How's that for snappy work! He says the monarchs have arrived at the marriage. That means they know in London that we've delivered our cargo safely."

CHAPTER

6

Roy and Jim lay on bumpy straw mattresses on the floor of the garret of the small two-story house, peering by day through a shuttered window onto the street, listening at night to the hobnailed boots of the enemy patrols passing every hour. This was their sole connection with the life of the outside world. For they were forbidden to go outdoors—even in the garden which was in the rear of the house—by day or by night. Most of the time, Marcel lay there with them, for he, of course, was in great danger, too.

They had come to Floreac in a high-wheeled peasant cart drawn by two horses, carrying a cow to the local slaughterhouse. Each was dressed as a farm hand in a dingy smock, wooden sabots on his feet, and a beret. On the road they passed a dozen

German patrols, the "Green Coats," as Marcel termed them disdainfully. He was without his machine gun, which he called his "sulphur sprayer," explaining that it was about the same size as the sprayers used to dust the vineyards of the locality during the season. Driving this cart through town, they had delivered the cow, after which Marcel had led them to a small bar in the neighboring square. Inside was a single customer, a man sitting at a table with a newspaper in his hand, who did not look at them. After a while he clicked a coin against the marble-topped table, summoned the ancient waiter, paid for his drink and departed. In five minutes they got up and left, too. Roy was amazed to find that the man was only a block away. He sauntered down a street, and they followed him at some distance. Along several back streets, through an alley, into a doorway in a garden wall, and so into the home of one of the inhabitants of Floreac. The first station on their journey.

The owner of the house was called Lucien Jacques. Whether that was his real name or his name in the Resistance, they never discovered. He was not called Monsieur Jacques, or Lucien, but always Lucien Jacques. He was an instructor **or** teacher in the local school, a tallish man, half bald, thin like everyone they met, with a queer, gray-colored face. His wife, small, active, also gray-faced and thin, cooked meals for all four men from the tiny rations at her disposal, made a somewhat un-appetizing soup and baked strange-looking bread. Occasionally also there was a tasteless vegetable called rutabaga, almost too tough to eat. During their stay of several weeks they did not look forward to meals in the home of Lucien Jacques.

During that time, however, they learned through their hosts, and thanks to Marcel's growing knowledge of English, something about the Resistance. Outside France, in the American Army, everyone talked about the Underground. Inside France, as they soon discovered, it was called the Resistance. One is in the Resistance, one makes the Resistance, one is a Resister. There were, in the Resistance, two kinds of people—the hard and the soft. That is, those who were tough and those who weren't. The *Maquis,* the men who lived in the country, those they had met in the inn the night of their crash, who remained in the hills and forests of the Dor-dogne, fighting the Germans whenever and wher-ever they could, were the pure Resistance. Then there were the "legal ones," people like Lucien Jacques and his wife, who were apparently ordinary civilians, yet were working all the time in the Resistance at home.

They would have to wait in Floreac, they learned, for word from headquarters of the Department to start them on their journey to the coast. The business of escaping from France was not, apparently, as easy once you were inside the country as it had seemed when being briefed in the Operations Tent before a night mission. Many other downed airmen, and many French Resisters, were anxious to get out also, and everyone had to wait his turn. A message, they found, would be sent when their turn arrived. Messages as a rule were unwritten; if written, they were placed in cigarette papers so they could be swallowed if necessary. Sometimes they were carried in bicycle tires or the lining of a man's necktie. Occasionally the messengers were women, and they heard of women who journeyed for miles by bicycle in mid-winter storms with messages. These messages were delivered to a friendly house in each town called a letter box. When discovered by the Germans, the people in the house were promptly shot, and the property burned to the ground. The letter box was then said to have been destroyed, and a new one had to be set up. This often meant a delay of several weeks.

A dozen, a hundred times a day during their sojourn in Floreac, Roy wished he had studied French at school, or at least tried to learn some words and phrases in the long months in North Africa and Corsica. Often he listened to conversations between Jim and Marcel, conducted partly in bad French, partly in bad English. Lucien Jacques and his wife frequently came up at night to join them. Slowly Roy realized what it was, this Resistance. And these Resisters. He learned of the children in school, so underfed that if sent to the blackboard they could not stand. These people, these pale, undernourished folk, did not look at all like heroes, but they were heroes. They risked their lives all day every day, they and thousands all over France.

There was Marcel's sister who thought it was fun to stand on the platforms of buses in Bordeaux and slip anti-German pamphlets in the pockets of enemy officers. Or his friend, the telephone clerk in Lyon, who went out regularly after curfew when it was death to be caught by a German patrol, to cut wires. Or the local postmaster, a wounded war veteran, who invariably managed to get his crutches entangled with officers' legs in the cafés; or the nephew of Lucien Jacques, a farm boy of twelve, who gave an armored column the wrong directions and sent them forty miles out of their way in the dark. Then there was the butcher in Floreac who had an argument with a German, lost his temper, and ended up by throwing the man into his refrigerator. No traces of the soldier were ever found, though everyone in town knew perfectly well what had happened.

Occasionally they got a small sheet of flimsy tissue paper, one of the Resistance newspapers called *Combat,* or *Libération.* Then Marcel would lie on his back translating the news laboriously. Through one of these sheets they learned that IT was approaching. IT was the landing, the famous landing, the landing promised the French for three years, and so long deferred, so long awaited, the moment for which the French, so many times deceived, hardly dared hope. One night, when they were listening to the radio which Marcel had carried along, with Madame Lucien Jacques at the window watching for German patrols in the street, a message came that sent the three French into ecstasy.

They suddenly jumped, half-shouting, talking excitedly together, all of them. Lucien Jacques immediately disappeared down the trap door to the ground floor. For some time the Americans were unable to understand what had happened. Then it became clear. The message had come from the B.B.C. in London, the message all France had waited for so many years.

Only six words. "The fairy has a lovely smile." Yet to the men and women of the Resistance it meant everything. Hold yourself in readiness; IT is at hand. Invasion! Release! Freedom is near. Lucien Jacques soon appeared at the trap door of the attic with a bottle and glasses in his hands. He held out the glasses to Marcel. That night the three French and the two Americans drank the last bottle of champagne left in the house.

They were cheered, all of them, knowing that deliverance was close. Roy, especially, felt happy. The pain in his leg and thigh was less severe. As the doctor predicted, the rest had helped. The pain returned sometimes, as when he knelt too long at the window watching for German patrols; but day by day it lessened. Soon he felt able to take whatever might come. Finally, late one evening, word arrived. They were to be ready to leave town the next day, traveling nearer the coast, mostly by small, local trains. Boarding an express meant more controls, more inspections, more danger.

Jim became Dennis Dupont, *cultivateur* or farm hand from Plessis, near Floreac. Roy was Georges Barraux, his cousin, a *vigneron* or wine grower from the region. They were journeying to the town of Dax to work for the summer with relatives. Identity cards, with their own pictures in French civilian clothes and stamped by a seal stolen from the German *Komandateur* of the town, were in order. Everything was fixed for the getaway.

Saying good-by to Madame Lucien Jacques, they left about ten the next morning. Out the back gate, down the alley, along rear streets to the station. Marcel carried an antique pasteboard suitcase that seemed to be falling apart. Walking along, they discovered that the radio was in the suitcase. It was one that had been brought in by Fried Spratt, and it was to be delivered at their next stop to someone in the Resistance. Looking down at the feeble suitcase, its handle tied with string, an old shirt sticking from a hole in one corner, Jim wondered how Marcel dared to carry it. He asked him about it.

"In the Resistance, is dangerous everytheeng. **To**

sleep, to eat, to live is dangerous. Wan day my sees-
ter in train puts valise with Resistance journals up
. . . so . . . above. It breaks, the valise. Down
come journals, dozens and dozens."

"What happened, Marcel?"

"Nawtheeng. The people in train, they know;
they peeck up journals and put back."

The two boys looked at each other, trusting no
such occurrence would happen on their trip. Now
they were nearing the *Place de la Gare*. There was
the station, with its stopped clock which said five
minutes to six. A German soldier, his bayonet on his
rifle, stood at the entrance. They brushed his sleeve
as they passed within. The waiting room was completely jammed, and a long line stood at the tiny
ticket window. People were milling round with bun-
dles, baggage, boxes, clothes tied up in sheets, and
one woman even had a live hen, its feet fastened by
a string, in a patent leather shopping bag. Both the
hen and the bag looked the worse for wear. Finally
Marcel got their tickets and came toward them,
perspiring visibly. At the train gate, the blue-coated
railwayman with the German officer beside him
punched their tickets and inspected their identity

cards carefully. Then he shoved them through and onto the platform.

Like the waiting room, the platform was a madhouse. Hundreds of expectant travelers stood in the space for a third that number. When the train arrived, an hour late, there was a terrific battle to get aboard. Marcel fought his way in, and they followed. Unlike our trains, each car was divided into little compartments running across the carriage, seating five on a side. The benches were of wood, hard and uncomfortable, especially when twelve people were jammed into the space for ten.

The train stayed forever in the station, but finally, giving a shriek, it pulled slowly away, leaving many would-be passengers stranded frantically on the platform. They moved through a warm, sunny countryside, a land of white stone houses with red roofs, many grapevines, farms with every inch of land cultivated. The tiny train, already overloaded, stopped at each station along the line, frequently unsnarling a few weary passengers and invariably taking on many more, who jammed themselves somehow into the corridor that was filled with baggage and people standing up or sitting on their suitcases. At about two in the afternoon, they reached a main junction where they had to change for the trip to Dax, their destination. Unfortunately here it was necessary to take an express.

Since they did not wish to pass the gate into the station and have their identity cards checked again by German sentries, they sat down on the stone platform to wait. Madame Lucien Jacques had given them a lunch of tough meat sandwiches and a bottle of wine. It was steaming hot, and they longed for water, but discovered that the water from the fountain at one end of the platform was not drinkable. The express was late, and it was nearly four in the afternoon before it thundered into the station. The coaches were completely full, and they were immediately assaulted by the same furious crowd of baggage-laden travelers. This time only Roy managed to get a tiny space in a compartment, while Jim and Marcel had to squeeze with a dozen others into the long corridor that ran down one side of the car.

Ten minutes after leaving, the French police came past. Roy felt perspiration on his forehead as a gendarme in the corridor touched his cap with one finger and leaned into the compartment. Another policeman checked the standees outside. The man at the door glanced hard at Roy, but returned his identity card without a word. Then he spoke to Marcel by the window in the passageway. His tones were low, yet excited. Marcel, in turn, immediately began whispering to Jim.

Something's about to break, Roy thought. If only I could understand what's going on!

The whole compartment was interested now; the two soldiers beside him with their guns between their feet; the old man with the waxed mustachios; the ancient lady at the window, with the voluminous skirts and the black velvet band round her neck; the worker with the beret; the young girl with the wicker basket on her knees, all of them. They understood what Roy did not.

Then Jim leaned over him into the compartment. "Gestapo! The Germans are following down the car below to check on the French police. They'll want your identity card. Whatever happens, don't talk."

Suddenly the ancient lady in the far corner leaned toward Roy across the seats.

"*Vous!*" She was pointing at him. "*Vous!* Spik French?"

Roy had been told by the Intelligence Officer at the base a dozen times that if brought down in

France he was to obey the orders of the Resistance. The orders of the Resistance came through Marcel, and they were that he was not to talk. So he did not talk. He simply shook his head.

Instantly the old lady began to make weird motions. She beckoned to him, she spread out her skirts, while the soldier next to him seized his arm and pointed toward her. Roy neither understood what they wanted nor what he should do. Then there was a scream, a horrible scream far down the car, a scream that rose above the noise and the jolting of the train; a woman's cry, tragic and lonely.

The whole compartment sat tense, listening. Then Roy was pulled and hauled over their feet toward the old lady beside the window. She motioned to him to get down, put her hand on his shoulder and yanked him to the floor. Extending her skirts, she enveloped him completely. From the young girl next to her she grabbed the wicker basket and placed it in her lap, just above Roy's head.

From the corridor outside came the sounds of a scuffle, harsh German tones, and the sobbing of a French woman as she was led from the car. Next Roy heard a sharp, short command in a guttural voice, and he could guess that they were all handing over their identity cards. The old lady's hand was on his shoulder, steadying him, patting his arm gently. He knelt there, desperately uncomfortable, his knees sore, his head hurting where the old lady pressed the wicker basket into his neck. The pain in his leg became acute again. His whole hip began to ache intolerably; it seemed impossible to stand his cramped position any longer. Then finally the harsh German voice moved to the next compartment.

The old lady waited a minute, moved the wicker basket off his head, lifted her skirts, and Roy climbed out, red of face, clenching his teeth as the pain stabbed up and down his leg. He squeezed into his seat at the other end of the compartment. No one said a word. The old lady was looking out the window.

For perhaps half an hour the train jolted along on a most uneven track. Jim leaned against the window of the corridor, but Marcel was not in sight. At last he appeared, smiling, hot and perspiring. Instantly Roy understood. The French police knew Marcel would be picked up by the German control that followed them along the corridor of the train, so they had hidden him somewhere until the inspection was finished.

CHAPTER

7

THE station at Dax was larger than the ones they had passed through during the day. The crowd was larger, too. Wedged securely in the mob, the three men trying to keep together in the event of trouble, they worked down the platform to where the huge exit sign hung overhead. There they anticipated an inspection of their identity cards. When they were near the gate, with no way of escape, they realized the German control party at the barrier was also searching everyone's baggage.

Since all radios were forbidden, and the one carried by Marcel was evidently of foreign make, discovery seemed inevitable.

There was no time to think. Already they were close to the exit gate, handing over their tickets to the French railway guard, and their false identity cards to the stolid German non-com with the rifle on his shoulder. Roy was ready to bolt through the mob and try to run for it, although he knew perfectly well that even should he succeed in getting outside the station, he would be picked up in town immediately.

They looked at each other. Next to Roy was Marcel, with the betraying suitcase in his hand. In front of him tottered a little girl of four or five, lugging a heavy bundle, a youngster thin-legged and weak like all the kids they had seen in France. She was trying to get through the gate. By Marcel's other elbow was a tall German soldier, evidently returning from leave at home. Suddenly Marcel thrust the suitcase at him, said a few words in French, picked up the little girl and her bundle, and went through the gate holding out his identity card. The official tore open the bundle which contained old clothes, and nodded for them to go on. Meanwhile, the soldier carrying the valise passed by without an inspection. Marcel put down the child and took the valise.

"*Merci, mon vieux,*" he said. The soldier smiled and moved along.

But they were not safe yet. Just beyond stood a

French policeman, a rifle slung over his back. He had observed the maneuver, and stepped forward. Taking Marcel roughly by the arm, he pointed to the suitcase, plainly asking what was in it. Once more Roy was desperate, getting set to run, to push through the mob into the street and safety outside. But again nothing happened. On tiptoe, Marcel reached up and whispered something to the tough gendarme. The man turned away. They were in the street.

Roy wiped his forehead. Gosh! And those Intelligence Officers used to claim this escape business was a setup if you did what you were told!

"What did you say to him, Marcel?"

The little Frenchman glanced round to be sure no one heard. "I take beeg chance. I say in valise is American radio for Resistance. O.K.!"

The station square was jammed with antique carriages drawn by bony horses, a few German jeeps, and one or two French automobiles with queer wood-burning engines attached at the back. Roy paused to stare at these contraptions, but Jim poked him sharply. They ducked down a side street into the poorer quarters of the town, past several blocks of flats. Then Marcel stopped at a small, unpreten-

tious house, like dozens of others in the neighbor-
hood. He looked around carefully, then knocked
hastily three times. There was a long moment or two
of waiting. Finally the door opened and they
stepped inside.

They were looking into a dim hallway. At the far
end of it was a sub-machine gun. Behind the gun
was a German soldier.

They stood there, too stunned to move.

The German fingered the gun as if he meant business.

Then an officer stepped from behind the door
with a Schmeiser machine pistol in his hand. He
barked a command. They didn't understand nor did
they need to. Silently they ranged themselves
against the wall. There they were all searched and
searched carefully by two soldiers under the watch-
ful eyes of the officer. Their identity cards were
found, glanced at, and tossed contemptuously on a
table. Marcel was led upstairs. The two Americans
were shoved into an adjoining room and the door
was locked behind them. A sentry paced back and
forth outside the only window.

Just when everything seemed to be working out,
when they had gone through two close shaves, when

they were almost there! Days of hiding, hours of living in constant danger, moments of agony as capture seemed inevitable—then this! Something had gone wrong, some slip had been made, and the station had been discovered by the enemy. What had actually happened they never knew; nor what became of Marcel, now their friend. They knew that he was probably being tortured in a room upstairs. Roy and Jim sat alone in the dusk, unable to speak, unable even to think, prisoners of the German Army. Or worse still, of the Gestapo.

At last the door opened and a sentry stood there. He beckoned to Jim, who rose, shook hands with Roy, and left. Then the door shut, and Roy could hear their footsteps down the hall. He was completely alone.

On the wall above him was a faded calendar. He got up and looked at it closely. May 30th. A holiday at home! Home, another world, another planet, another existence; something millions of miles from this grim room, and the German sentry pacing up and down in the garden outside, and imprisonment or death or something even more unpleasant to follow. He tried to concentrate upon home and things of home. The Germans had taken his wrist watch with the rest of his belongings, but he knew it was a little after six o'clock. Allowing for the five hours' difference in time between Europe and the eastern part of the United States, it would be a little past one in the afternoon at home. This was Decoration Day, the first really warm day of the year, and the ball park would be filling fast now. The sounds and cries of the scorecard men and the peanut vendors would be coming from the stands. The pitchers would be burning in their warm-ups behind the plate, and the umpires, chest protectors under their arms, would be strolling out together from the clubhouse. Home, Decoration Day, a double-header to come and the stands full all over the land. And here . . . now . . .

The door opened suddenly. There stood the sentry, nodding to him curtly. He rose and went out. Now for it!

The German led him to the front room again where two officers were seated. They told him in crisp English to step forward. The sentry remained two paces to the rear, the machine gun on his arm. Jim was not to be seen.

The forged papers lay on the table in front of the officers. They were young, good-looking, not in the least what he had imagined the typical German officer to be. They looked him over for a minute, asking him some perfunctory questions in perfect English—questions about his name, age, grade, and so on. To all he replied truthfully.

Then one officer said: "Sergeant, when were you brought down in France? And where?"

Roy was by no means sure of the correct answers to these queries. He was only sure of one thing—that he must give them no useful information. So he said nothing.

"Where is your squadron based at present? Still on Corsica?"

Again he remained silent. Question followed question. What was the strength of the 12th Airforce? How long had he been overseas? Where? With what outfit? To every question he refused to reply.

Finally one officer said something in German, and the sentry clicked his heels, turned round, and left the room. The other officer rose and went out by a door in the rear. Roy was now alone with the elder man at the table. His knees were quivering curiously.

"Sit down." There was a chair behind him, and

Roy sat, quickly. The German rose. He was tall, agreeable, dressed in a well-cut uniform. His yellow hair was plastered back over his head, and he smelled faintly of some kind of lotion as he came round the table and seated himself on the edge, facing his prisoner.

He spoke quietly. "Doubtless you are aware of your position, sergeant. You are a prisoner of war, caught in civilian clothes. You can be shot. We do not intend to do this. Nor will the German Army, which respects the rules of warfare and adheres to the Geneva Convention, maltreat you in any way. Do you understand that?"

Sure I do, Roy thought. But what are you getting at? Aloud he said, "Yes, sir."

"Quite. But you are alone in this room, alone with me. Now we are determined to find out about your stay in France with these communists. We intend to stamp out lawlessness of all kinds. For the last time, do you care to answer my questions?"

Roy remained silent. Now for it! What'll I do? How shall I behave? He remembered poor Marcel telling them of an artist friend of his in the Resistance who was being tortured by the Gestapo. One night, fearful he would break down, that he would be unable to hold out any more, he tore up his shirt and hanged himself in his cell.

Roy fingered the thin shirt he wore.

The German rose. "I am regretful, sergeant. I am indeed very sorry. It is the business of this bureau to obtain information." He leaned back, and from a top drawer in the desk took out one of the most angry-looking knives Roy had ever seen. It was perhaps ten or twelve inches long, with both blades sharpened, something like the knives that were carried by the Special Service Force and other shock troops.

"The German Army, sergeant, does not harm prisoners. However . . . obviously . . . we are alone in this room. Were I attacked by a prisoner, I should, of course, defend myself. If you were hurt, there would be no one here . . . you understand. I mean, if I defend myself . . ."

Roy understood. With horror he watched the man stand. He was tall, towering above the chair where Roy sat. Now he raised the knife and came forward one step.

It was not courage that saved Roy. It was fear. For he was unable to move. Or speak. He sat rigid and silent, watching the knife.

For a minute that seemed endless, the German stood there, ready to strike. Then with an oath he turned abruptly, and flung the knife in exasperation upon the table. He was swearing in German, angry at his failure to obtain any information. Roy still sat motionless, his forehead wet, his knees shaking. Then there was a loud command. The sentry entered and tapped him on the shoulder.

For a few seconds he was unable to rise. It was hard to stand, harder still to totter out the door. On a bench in the hallway sat Jim, haggard, his hands in manacles. His worried eyes were on Roy, who slipped down, exhausted and empty, by his side.

CHAPTER

8

THEY did not sleep well that night in their dirty cell in the old stone prison of Dax. One does not sleep well with handcuffs on one's wrists, nor yet after the strain of such a day as they had endured.

For a week they were kept there with nothing to eat but a horrible soup twice daily. Then, early one morning, they were marched under guard to the railway station and put aboard a train. They were locked into a third class compartment together with two Canadian aviators, a British commando, and a Polish flying officer, all handcuffed like themselves. After the loneliness of the stone cell, it was heaven to be outside, to talk with these others, even though everyone realized they were heading north for a German prison camp.

Most of the morning was spent shifting their car

round the yards. Hungry, sore, hopeless, they were a dispirited lot. Then, just before noon, a dreadful sight passed their window. In three open box cars were some hundreds of young men, packed in so closely they could not sit down. Their heads were shaved, they were manacled. But they were not sorry for themselves. Instead they were singing defiantly as they moved, ultimately to be sent as slave labor to the north. As their cars came abreast of the compartment, the Frenchmen saw the foreigners and shouted and yelled with vehemence. Some even tried to raise their manacled hands and wave.

"What's that!" exclaimed one of the Canadians suddenly. He stepped clumsily on Roy's feet as he leaped to the window, calling to the French, talking to them with excitement in his voice as the cars slid past. Then he turned back to the men in the compartment.

"It's the Invasion! They say the Allies landed this morning in Normandy."

They were stunned. Invasion! Invasion at last! Could it be true? Was it just another rumor, like so many others, a rumor that like the rest would be proved false in the end? All through the long, hot day, when sleep was impossible, they discussed the story. Jim told of the B.B.C. message they had heard in Floreac, and how it affected their hosts. The Polish flying officer was sure, from certain orders given his squadron, that the day was fixed for the 6th of June. Today was the 6th.

In the afternoon the train, with the box cars in the rear, pulled slowly out of the station of Dax, and moved through miles of pine forests. They would travel at a slow clip for perhaps half an hour, then be shunted off to a siding to permit long troop trains of German soldiers to roar past. Whenever they paused, snatches of song came from those cars in the rear.

Dusk came, then night, and still talk of the invasion continued in their compartment. At every station they went through, sentries patrolled the tracks, and they could feel excitement in the air among the enemy troops. Then it grew late. Despite their manacled hands and empty, aching stomachs, fatigue conquered them one by one. They slept.

It was sometime toward the middle of the night or early morning when, without warning, the train came to a wickedly abrupt stop with a jerk that threw them all together in confusion. There were no lights in the compartment, and they could see

nothing outside as they picked themselves up, groping for their seats. Then there was a shot. Another
shot. The rat-tat-tat of a machine gun could be
heard somewhere up front. Outside in the corridor
of their car German guards raced past, barking
commands in loud tones and firing through the
windows into the blackness.

All at once a face appeared at their window in
the moonlight, a head with a beret on. The man
spoke sharply, saying something in quick French.

The Canadian instantly understood and took command. "It's the *Maquis!* They've stopped the train.
Quick, let's go! Hurry there, lieutenant! You're next,
sergeant. Then you, captain. Hurry . . ."

Roy climbed with difficulty out of the window
just as the door of their compartment was unlocked
and a German voice shouted at them. Outside and
near him a gun exploded, and he heard a shriek and
the sound of a heavy body falling to the corridor
floor. Clumsily he let himself down to the ground,
helped by two men below, for the distance was
about eight feet.

Someone then grabbed his arm and pointed toward a flashlight sparkling through the woods. He
limped toward it as fast as he could, forgetting his

back and his aching leg, stumbling over the ties, while machine guns kept sputtering at intervals up and down the track. Then there was an explosion when someone tossed a hand grenade at one of the front cârs, and in a minute a crackling flame mounted as the woodwork of the coach caught fire.

Roy kept jogging along. Every few yards men with machine guns crooked in their arms protected his journey and directed him where to go. The *Maquis* had the attack well organized. The French boys from the box cars, who were able to make better time, were swarming past him now. Up and down the long train men were dropping from every window. Only in the front carriage, which evidently carried a strong armed guard, was there still any opposition.

Once Roy tripped and fell, then picked himself up and went on until he reached a country road, crossing the track some distance ahead of the engine. Trucks were parked all along the road in the dark. Nothing had been left to chance; nothing was unprovided for. There were even men with keys and others with hacksaws to cut their manacles or unfasten them. With a dozen other escaped prisoners, Roy swung himself slowly and with difficulty up the side of one of the trucks. Somebody from below gave him a welcome boost. Now that it was over or almost over, he was conscious of the agonizing pain in his leg.

But he was free again—with the invasion started up north and Allied troops slowly moving toward them. The truck ahead roared, rocked, and moved off. The sound of fighting around the front of the train increased, continued, and then slowly subsided. The glare from the burning car became lower and lower. More men clambered over the side of the truck. Roy could tell the fighting was ending by the way the machine-gun fire slackened. Shouts, cries in German, and quick bursts of fire came to him through the wood. Apparently the *Maquis* took no prisoners.

There was a jolt. The truck started, tumbling them all over on each other in a heap. It moved through the soft-smelling pine woods, gaining speed slowly. He was free again.

CHAPTER
9

Up ahead, the big *Queen* loomed above the long line of men—wounded, disabled, and casuals who were going on board her. The line seemed never to move, and Roy thought how glad he would be when this standing in line was finished and done with.

Yet move it did, inch by inch, slowly, steadily, always under the glare of those powerful lights from overhead. Although it took several hours, eventually he reached a group of soldiers headed by a non-com with a long sheet of paper in his hand. They were standing beside a desk, checking names.

Suppose my name isn't there! Suppose after all that someone has made a mistake! Suppose . . .

Then the non-com with the paper shouted at the corporal opposite, who bawled back:

"Tucker, Sergeant Roy, casual, six four one eight five three four. O.K."

That's me! Tucker, Sergeant Roy, casual, six four one eight five three four.

He slung the barracks bag, which got heavier every minute, onto his back again, and went up. It bumped the rail and hindered him as he mounted. His left hip ached terribly from the long period of standing in line, but he plugged along, up, up, up. Nothing mattered, nothing counted now. His name was on the list. He was going at last!

At the top another non-com made another name check. Once more someone bawled back:

"Tucker, Sergeant Roy, casual, six four one eight five three four. O.K."

A square blue card was thrust into his hand by an M.P. at one side. There were M.P.'s everywhere. They pointed out the way to go, showing the blue arrows overhead that led to his compartment. Close to the top of each staircase was an M.P. At the end of every corridor was an M.P. Down, down, along narrow aisles, down staircases, along more aisles, with that barracks bag now weighing two hundred pounds at least. At last he began to reach the bunks, tier after tier of them, feet swinging from every end.

Then an M.P. grabbed his arm. "In there! Fling it where you can, soldier."

Roy dropped the heavy barracks bag with relief and sank down. He needed badly to stretch out, to take the load off his feet, to relax and rest that aching hip. With some difficulty he climbed into the bunk, six feet six inches long and hardly wide enough to hold him. Only two inches separated Roy from the man next door, while a space of ten inches was between his heaving chest and the sag in the canvas made by the occupant overhead. Then, just as he got settled, just as he got stretched out, a voice came over the loudspeaker:

"Attention all personnel! Attention all personnel! At eleven hundred hours every morning there will be emergency muster on deck. All personnel will proceed to the nearest deck carrying life jackets which must be put on and properly tied. No smoking anywhere during emergency muster and inspection."

At that moment, an officer came along with a squad of soldiers. Roy was "hot flunked," meaning that he shared his bunk with another enlisted man; sleeping in turns, one night on deck, the next in the bunk below. He was to start on deck first. So, his aching leg rebellious, he began the endless climb to the top deck above.

"Hey there, soldier, your life belt," someone shouted after him. "Must carry that life belt all the time."

He reached out, grabbed it, and jammed along the packed corridors, up endless stairways, down narrow passages to the deck. Like everything else on ship, the deck was crowded; yet somehow he managed to squeeze in among the snoring hundreds on the hard planks and stretch out, covering himself with his coat and using the gray kapok life belt as a pillow. The deck was no soft mattress, and it was exactly where he would spend three nights out of their six at sea.

Never mind, boy, no matter; you're on board, you're going home!

The men around all had blue cards, too. For the ship was divided into three areas—the red (forward) area where the nurses and Red Cross girls lived; the white (midships) area where the officers were housed; and the blue (stern) area for enlisted men. No one, not even a colonel, could leave his designated area without permission. If he did, one of the seven hundred M.P.'s aboard made sure he got quickly back where he belonged.

There was a sudden piercing shriek from the ship's whistle overhead, a noise which startled even the soundest sleeper and the most weary soldier. Everyone sat up. Then Roy realized that the snuffling and puffing at the rear of the ship came from a couple of harbor tugs. Despite his aching leg, he rose and found his way to the rail.

Ten stories below, three tugs poured smoke from their funnels. They were backed up to the side of the ship just forward of the stern. Then there was a ripple, a tremor, the merest tremble in the deck at his feet. Oh, boy, there we go! The gangplanks were up, and ten stories down the Negro soldiers on the pier loosed the last lines from the bollards. They stood looking up enviously in the electric light. Poor guys, he thought. I'm going; you're staying. How many times will they see the big boat leave before they board her for good, too?

We're moving at last! No, not yet. Yes, we are, too. He fixed his eyes upon a post on the dock, and almost imperceptibly it slid past. The ship was leaving the dock, a few inches, a foot. Then the next post went by more quickly.

Yes, sir, we're really off! Well, he thought to himself, this is the moment, the thing a soldier dreamed about in the mud and filth and cold of Algiers, in the heat and the mosquitoes of Casamozza back there on Corsica, the thing he had thought about every night on those missions over Austria and Italy. That he was almost frightened to think about when they crashed in France; that he never dared carry in his consciousness when the Gestapo picked him up, when he was handcuffed with Jim in that clammy cell of the stone prison of Dax. Now it's here, here at last. The engines are turning, we're moving, we're really going.

Somewhere down on the pier a military band started playing "God Bless America." In the murky darkness fifteen thousand soldiers sang, sang intensely as they had never sung before.

Once it was just a song, a tune with words about your country. Now it was different. You'd been overseas twenty-two months, you'd seen something and lived through a few things since you left home. A few things you'd rather forget. So you sang it with a new meaning.

Now the dock was farther away, and the black stevedores on the pier were indistinct figures.

No mistake, the big ship was really trembling now, no mistake about it. The engines were turning at last. Toot-toot, toot-toot, toot-toot went the tug at the stern as a kind of salute. Toot-toot, toot-toot, toot-toot went a tug on the other side.

Good-by, England, land of warm beer and warm, friendly people. Good-by!

Roy stood at the rail in the deep sunshine, watching the blue Atlantic swish past sixty feet below, until his leg ached all the way from the hip. Or he sat tailor-fashion on the deck, or else lay on his stomach propped on his elbows until they hurt and he had to shift his position. The only comfortable posture was stretched out flat on his back. Then he was free from that intolerable toothache in his leg, and only then. Unfortunately, on the big *Queen,* her decks brown with uniformed humanity, space was not easy to find topside.

Anyhow, I'm going home. This isn't the unknown; it's not subs and danger and a war ahead. This is home, and the things we know. It's thirty knots, full speed ahead.

As the great ship rose and fell in the gentle swell

of the Atlantic, every second meant a few yards nearer New York. Already he felt the influence of home—the news in the ship's paper, with the baseball scores in detail, and the food, especially the good American food. As a man in the chow line next to Roy remarked: "Boy! It must *rain* milk in that-there country."

For the first time in twenty-two months, Roy had all the milk he wanted, and American coffee. At breakfast there was fruit—real fruit, not juice from a can, and bacon and eggs—real eggs, not an omelet made from powdered eggs. And liver and sausages if you wished, also. As only two meals were served aboard ship, Roy made a sandwich of a piece of ham, wrapped it in a paper napkin, and shoved it into his pocket to hold him over until dinner at 4:30. Dinner meant more American food—soup, roast beef, vegetables, salad, ice cream, and coffee again —all he could eat of it.

On deck he scrounged a place, took a detective yarn, and tried hard to make himself comfortable with a blanket and a life belt for a pillow. All day long he listened to the conversation around him.

"Where ya from, soldier?"

"Omaha, Nebraska."

"Omaha! Ain't never seen it. But if it's like Omaha, France, if it's like that beach, you can have it, brother."

"Boy, when I get home, know what I'm gonna do? First off, I'm gonna turn in and say to my Ma: 'Ma, don't wake me up, not if I sleep till next Christmas. Don't wake me.'"

"The Jerries was over here . . . on this hill to our right, see? And Sam, his platoon was coming through the woods on our left, when they started to give us the works."

"Remember that bottle of champagne he liberated in Lyons, remember that, Sid?"

It was the third day out that the familiar question came, the one he had heard so often during his service in the Army, the one he dreaded now because of the questions that invariably followed. It came, as it always came, out of a clear sky for no reason at all. Just a bunch of soldiers sitting in a circle talking, when one man asked casually, "Hey, soldier, you ain't by any chance the Tucker usta play center field for the Dodgers, are ya?"

"Yeah, guess *so.*"

"You are!" Immediately a crowd formed. A second before he was only another Air Force sergeant.

Now he was someone, a celebrity, the man who led the National League in batting the year before the war.

"Say! You Roy Tucker!"

"Not *the* Roy Tucker!"

"Say . . ."

"D'you guess the Dodgers'll win this year?"

"How's the Cards look to ya, fella?"

"Are you going to get back in this summer?"

A dozen, a hundred questions were tossed at him. They were the same questions he always heard, and he could answer them in his sleep. All except one.

"Yeah . . . Nope . . . I guess . . . Sure is a sweet ballplayer . . . They're a right fast outfit . . . Looks like we'll have to go some to win this year . . . Dunno if I'll make the grade or not."

That was all Roy could say to the last question. But there was plenty more he could think. How does a guy with a leg like this play baseball? And if I can't, what then? Suddenly as he talked to the crowd around him, his hands were wet with sweat.

Time passed slowly, but eventually came the last, the final night aboard. Roy found it impossible to sleep that night; so did fifteen thousand other soldiers, as the *Queen* churned through the smooth seas off the coast. At four A.M. the loudspeakers blared forth, but few men were asleep. After breakfast, Roy lugged his bursting barracks bag up topside, just in time to see a lightship slide past them in the dimness of breaking dawn. Suddenly a cluster of lights twinkled far to their right. It was America!

They didn't yell or cheer or shout. A strange hush fell over the big *Queen* packed with soldiers from stem to stern. They said nothing; they just stood looking at those lights in the murky mist, everyone solemn and quiet. It was too immense for words. Boy, there she is!

Sunrise came, and the far rim of the horizon became shoreline, and the shoreline showed tiny houses and a green bank and an army fort with the flag flying above. A white transport launch poked through the mist. The men yelled, and a few WACS and Red Cross Girls aboard the launch waved back and kidded the soldiers. The shoreline was distinct now, and there were autos, real autos, and streets and people and houses intact, not smashed into rubble.

Slowly the ship glided into the upper harbor. "Hey, guys, look! Look, there's the Old Lady, off there to the left. See?"

Golden shafts of early morning sunshine etched the Statue of Liberty. "Yep, there she is. Got kinda fat, too, since we left," remarked a jokester.

Every whistle in the harbor was tied down as the *Queen*, doing about six knots, came up the lower bay. She was greeted by the sirens from the shore and the ferryboats laden with commuters who thronged the rails and waved. Then up ahead was the most gorgeous sight of all. Suddenly through that morning mist came the white towers of Manhattan, fairy towers, reaching into the sky, their lower parts still concealed in the haze. Boats with flags flying, giving three sharp whistle salutes, came alongside. Each one carried a band. The men on the packed decks shrieked approval.

Now the loudspeaker began blaring out commands. "All Silver Star men report to forward promenade deck gangway. They will be the first to leave."

"Hey, Tuck, that's you! Hey there, report to the forward promenade deck, all Silver Star men, didn't ya hear?"

Aw, what's that mean! I'd rather go off with the boys.

"Blue cards will debark for Camp Shanks, leaving

[81]

by ferry from the pier. Red cards will entrain for Camp Kilmer immediately following debarkation."

Now the *Queen* was almost opposite the Whitehall Building at the tip of Manhattan. The ship had slowed down, and Roy felt the intense heat of a New York summer day. Horns, whistles, sirens, from both the New York and Brooklyn sides, drowned out the bands, deafened one with their noise. Hoots, toots, and short shrieks of welcome came from the tugs and tankers, from the freighters anchored up the river, from the railroad engines over on the Jersey side. A Navy blimp flew overhead. Behind them was an ancient Sandy Hook boat, waiting to take off the seriously wounded.

We're home! Cripes, I can't somehow realize it. I can't believe it's me, that I'm home at last. Home, and I thought I'd never see it again.

Suddenly the pain in Roy's leg became so intense he had to sit down and rest for a few minutes. He had been standing in that excitement for several hours. What'm I gonna do? A ballplayer with a bum leg, what use is he to a club?

The tugs were taking up the ship's lines for berthing. Now they warped her gently against the pier, holding her flush with the slow tide and bringing

her slowly round, four, six, eight, ten of them, puffing and blowing. Roy rose and, looking over someone's shoulder, saw the long gangplank ready with
a mat at the bottom, and on the mat a map of the
United States with the word HOME on it. Now the
pier was close, and WACS and Red Cross girls and
lots of brass were waving at them from the second
story. And a band was playing "Take Me Out to
the Ballgame."

The men were singing, every single one. *"Buy
me some peanuts and crackerjack . . ."*

But what use is a guy with a bum leg to a ballclub?

"I don't care if I never come back."

The boys round about were shouting at him. "Hey
there, Roy! Hey, Tuck!" They turned from the rail
to yell, "Hi, Tucker, that's you! That's you, kid."

Yeah, that's me all right.

*"For it's one . . . two . . . three strikes you're
out . . . at the old . . . ballgame."*

Yeah, that's me. *Maybe* it's me.

CHAPTER

11

Roy dumped his barracks bag on a cot in a tent in Company 24A, and glanced around. Everywhere was the same hubbub and confusion he remembered in the Reception Center at Camp Upton where he had entered the Army four long years before. Here, however, the atmosphere was quite different. At Camp Upton one felt the aching loneliness of hundreds of men, many away from home for the first time in their lives, and one could see the distrust and dislike they felt at being herded in with strangers of every kind, at the promiscuity, the lack of privacy which came to some of them as a shock. Here this had all vanished. You were used to the Army, to strange companions; you took them as they came. There was none of the antagonism he remembered in the faces of the men in the Reception Center years before. At Fort Dix you understood each other without speaking.

A city block away, down near Eighth Street, the loudspeaker was going full blast. From it were issued all orders about the roster. At Fort Dix, the one item of primary importance was the roster, because you could not be processed for discharge until you got on the roster. "Are you on the roster yet?" "How long does it take a guy to get on the roster, bud?"

Apparently it took anywhere from two days to two weeks to get on the roster. Yet one had to listen carefully all day to the loudspeaker, for if your name was called and you failed to appear for processing, you might have to wait a week or more to get on the roster again.

That evening Roy wandered into a movie about the Pacific, where it was easy to tell the soldiers who had served there by the shouts and jeers that rose. Then he went to the PX for a beer. He stood there, drinking, watching the crowd, when someone called his name.

"Roy! Hey there, Tuck!"

He turned quickly. "Earl! You old so-and-so! How are you?"

"Boy, this is good! How are *you?*"

"Me? I'm swell; at least I think so. How'd you guys ever get out of France?"

"Kid, we climbed the Pyrenees, and lemme tell you something. They're six times higher'n the Himalayas. It was rugged and no fooling. Say, we heard when we got to England that you and Jim had been picked up by the Jerries in France. That right?"

"That's correct. We were picked up all right, chucked into the coldest, dampest jail I ever hope to see. Then they started to send us into Germany, and we were rescued by the *Maquis* from a train on the night of D-Day. They hid us until the 7th Army worked up from the south and overran the place."

"Yeah? So? What then?"

"Oh, the usual thing. England for a few weeks, and then I came back on the *Queen*."

"Ya did, hey! We come back on a freighter, the *Kokomo Victory*. But really, kid, how are you now? Does your leg bother you still? Will they let you go back to the ballclub this summer? They could sure use you to plug up that hole out in the field, couldn't they?"

"Oh, it doesn't bother me so much at present. I

spent the winter at the Greenville Army Air Base in South Carolina, and believe me, I took care of myself and rested."

They talked until lights out. The next morning Roy changed his tent to one in B Street, near Earl's and closer to the loudspeaker. Nothing happened all day as he listened. The next morning was also without incident, and then suddenly at 4:30 in the afternoon, he sat up.

"Roster eighteen dash thirty. Private first class George Wolheim, four three eight six three nine one. Corporal Edward T. Meltzer, nine six four one seven one seven. Sergeant Roy Tucker, six four one eight five . . ."

He jumped from his cot, listening to those familiar words. ". . . Will report to the Operations Tent tomorrow at 0-eight hundred for processing."

Well, here we go. I'm on the roster and it won't be long now.

But everyone was nervous. The man in the next cot, a quiet, elderly man, suddenly burst out: "I'm worried about that physical. If you slip up, they're likely to keep you here for weeks." And an Air Corps boy remarked: "Don't get mixed up, that's the main thing. Don't ask questions about your insurance or your back pay or anything. If you do, boy, you're really here for life."

"I hear they can hold you as essential if you use a typewriter or can add figures. Thank heaven, I can't."

They wouldn't be likely to hold a ballplayer, Roy thought. But he shared in the general nervousness, and slept little that night.

It was cold and rainy the following morning. A strong northeast wind drove the rain in squally gusts across the field east of his tent, whipping at the canvas and pelting the tent roof noisily. Someone suggested it was the tail end of the hurricane that Florida was getting. They were all ready for breakfast half an hour too early, and when it was there, Roy found he had no appetite and was far from anxious to eat. He returned to his tent, awaiting the call for Group eighteen dash thirty. It came just before eight o'clock, and he hustled over to the Operations Tent, lining up in the mud and rain in a column of twos under a soldier guide, who first called the roll to be sure everyone was present. The chap next to Roy had been scratched from the roster three times for not showing up or arriving late, and as a consequence it had taken him three weeks to get back on again.

First they were marched to the Post Theatre, where with several other groups they were given a talk by the chaplain. "Please go directly to your homes. Lots of men from other parts of the country hang around New York and blow in their money. Then we have telephone calls from home about them. There are many pitfalls between Fort Dix and your home, remember that, boys."

"Wish he'd give me the phone number of a couple of good pitfalls," said a wag near Roy. But this was a serious thing, and Roy was far too nervous to laugh. They were marched next to the Counseling Building several blocks away, where as usual they waited for their records to arrive. Just before noon, Roy's name was called, and he stepped forward to sit down across from a soldier at a small desk. The soldier looked over his records, checked them, asked what he had done in civilian life, and before Roy had finished explaining that he was a professional baseball player, out came the inevitable question.

"Say! You ain't Roy Tucker of the Dodgers, are ya? Ya are? Well, we'll hustle you through, boy. Them guys can use you out in the field right now."

He went to work immediately on Roy's records. "Any disabilities, fella? O.K. Insurance all set? Fine. Fill this out, Form A100, your work-record form. A job waiting? I'll say, and do they need you over there in Ebbets Field!" The soldier grinned cheerfully.

Roy only wished he was as certain about that waiting job as his questioner. It was all finished in a few minutes, and next the gang marched to the clothing supply building, where he drew a blouse, shirt, trousers, and new shoes. In an adjoining room, a WAC sewed on the golden discharge emblem with the eagle, "the homing pigeon" in Army parlance. Then to the medics.

This was what Roy had been dreading. It began in that usual atmosphere of sweating, naked bodies, with everyone stripping to shorts, socks, and shoes. A technician in a white apron measured his chest. Then an X-ray plate in a dark room was flattened against him. "Say 99. 99. 99." Boy, I'd sure like a nickel for every time I've said 99 in this man's army.

In the next room, Group eighteen dash thirty went in turn to three medical officers, each at a desk. More questions, a dental examination, and a squint by a captain down throat, ears, nose. After that an eye-testing chamber. His vision was perfect. Next his blood pressure was taken, then his pulse, and he was weighed.

A doctor took him into a cubbyhole and tested him for rupture. Another medic at a table glanced over his service record and began to ask questions.

"Any wounds, injuries or diseases contracted in the service?"

"H'm. I see you were brought down in France and sustained a back injury. That right?"

"Yes, sir."

"Bang you up some, did it?"

"Yessir, just a bit."

"How you feel at present?"

"Oh, I'm O.K. Never felt better in my life." It was the truth, too.

The doctor wasn't satisfied. He had Roy bend over and touch the floor. "Left you with considerable stiffness in that lumbar region, didn't it? Here . . . let me feel that back of yours."

Reluctantly Roy submitted to the doctor's fingers. Would he be sent back to a hospital? Would the doctor find an injury sufficient to keep him from obtaining his discharge?

"You been on active duty in Greenville all winter, sergeant?"

"Yes, sir."

"What sort of work were you doing?"

"Well, major, I was in the control tower at Greenville for a few months; then they had me working in the Base office."

"I see. You had no ill effects, no trouble at all with that back of yours? No pains, no record of hospitalization since you've been back in this country?"

"No, sir," replied Roy truthfully. What he didn't talk about was that constant ache in his leg.

The doctor stood looking. "H'm . . ." He ran his fingers up and down Roy's back, pressed him over toward the floor. Then he went round to the desk and wrote something upon Roy's service record. It was evident that he was making a notation of the stiffness for future reference. Then he nodded, and Roy hastily escaped. That finished the day, and as far as he was concerned it was enough.

When the bugle sounded the next morning, he woke with a start. This is the day! At eight came the call for Group eighteen dash thirty. Again they formed in a column of twos and were marked off to be paid. But things had been going too well. The rain had been pouring down all night, and now they discovered what was meant by the famous Fort Dix mud. It leaked into their shoes; the rain seeped through their raincoats. They stood outside the building, wet, angry, impatient. But there was nothing to do.

They stood there until lunch, when they slogged to the mess hall through the oozy mud, and then back again. The place was locked and the personnel gone to eat, so again there was nothing to do but wait grimly in the downpour. Shortly after one, a private first class entered with an armful of service records. One hour later they were called inside and told to form in line. At last the call had come for Group eighteen dash thirty.

Everyone was lined up at a desk and told to sign three copies of their discharge, two in ink and one in indelible pencil. The records were then taken to the other end of the room, where a chap impressed their thumbs on an inked glass plate and transferred the impression to their discharges.

So to the Finance Building to be paid. Fortunately they could wait inside, for there was another delay of forty minutes here. Then their group was called to go through a small, numbered gate, where

Roy signed his name on a pay roster and walked to a window to receive cash. What followed was the most aggravating hour of his life. Everything was ready. They were all but separated from the Army. Almost civilians. A big sign on the door ahead told them to "Move to Next Building for Farewell Speech and Discharge." But the man first in line at the pay window was short seven dollars and sixty cents. Moreover, he was determined to get it.

He was a thin, bespectacled boy with the infantry combat badge on his chest and plenty of service ribbons also. He leaned against the window, talking interminably with the harassed clerk inside, while the line lengthened and men started cracking jokes. After twenty minutes the jokes became sour. Someone back of Roy suggested they take up a collection for the bird. But he remained, leaning against the window, shaking his head.

Time passed. Men behind Roy rolled up their sleeves and cursed the chap at the window in loud tones. He paid no attention. Officers appeared behind the counter, checking the man's service record, referring to long lists of figures. Endlessly it went on, as the remarks from the long line to the rear grew hotter and hotter. Then there were sudden cheers.

A finance colonel came round outside and took the recalcitrant soldier into his private office to straighten things out. Roy stepped up. He was handed a check for $89.60 and fifty dollars in cash. The rest of his mustering-out pay was to be sent home. It amounted to almost a thousand dollars.

Now it was nearly five. Group eighteen dash thirty assembled outside the Finance Building in the rain, and were marched to a church several blocks away. An organ was playing as they came in. When the church was full, and everyone was seated on the wooden benches, a chaplain rose and said a short prayer. Then a lieutenant-colonel gave them their last army talk. He was there to say good-by as a representative of the Armed Services, to ask them to be good citizens as they had been good soldiers, and to thank them on behalf of their commander-in-chief. Next came those wonderful, those blessed words: "You will now step forward when your name is called to receive your honorable discharges."

For the last time he heard his name called. "Sergeant Roy Tucker, six four one eight five three four."

Roy stood, stepped forward, and saluted. He grasped the hand of the chaplain, who handed him his discharge in a large manila envelope. Then they filed out, moved despite themselves by the ceremony. The rain had stopped. The sun was shining in the west. He stood in the muddy street, unable to believe that he was really out of the Army at last.

12

Roy spent two months with his grandmother on the farm at home. The Dodgers were hopelessly in the ruck of the pennant race, with no chance whatever of being a contender. Roy had written Jack Mac-Manus, owner of the club, that he would report in Brooklyn later in the summer. So for some weeks he merely lay around, content to be out of the Army and doing nothing, far from orders and commands and reveille at 5:45 A.M. every morning. He slept, he rested and lay in the sunshine. Occasionally he tested his leg. The stiffness in his hip seemed to be lessening, and only when he made quick starts and stops did the pain return. Finally he felt like visiting Ebbets Field.

It didn't take long to discover that whereas he was only a sergeant with a number in the Army, he was something special in Brooklyn. A bright-eyed kid, one of a gang lined up at the bleacher windows, spotted him, and immediately he was surrounded by half a hundred autograph seekers asking half a hundred questions simultaneously. Old Jake, the attendant at the player's gate, saw him coming and greeted him with an enormous grin, and his journey to the dugout was a triumphal procession. Every ten feet someone stopped him to shake hands; everywhere were smiling faces. Now he was back with his gang again.

It was good to see these old friends, to realize by their expression how glad they were to have him back once more. They made this plain, all of them, by the way their faces lighted with pleasure at his approach, by their firm handshakes and those heartening slaps on his back. It was good to be out there on the field, to hear again the sounds of the game he loved; the slap-slap, slap-slap of ball and glove, the shouts and cries from the stands, the familiar voices of the players in the field. He could scarcely believe he was in that accustomed spot, in the spike-scarred dugout, looking once more over the green turf.

"Boy, it's hard to believe. No fooling, I can't really believe I'm back!"

"Hello there, Spike! Glad to see you, Mr. Mac. Yessir, I'm sure anxious to get into that monkey suit again. Hello there, Al. Hi, Razzle! Say, this is great, Raz. Hello, Charlie, old boy."

It was grand to see the old gang, what was left. For many had gone. Bob Russell was on Guam with the Navy; Jocko Klein was in Germany; Alan Whitehouse was playing baseball for the Army on the coast; Harry Street was back in the States after receiving injuries with the 4th Marines at Tarawa; and Bones Hathaway was still in England.

It was good to see the men he knew; Swanny and Fat Stuff and Razzle. But it wasn't the Dodgers he remembered, this sixth-place ballclub. It seemed like a different outfit.

No wonder there was a new furrow in the forehead of Spike Russell, the manager. Swanny had been moved in from right field and stationed at third. Many of the pitchers, all the catchers, and the whole outfield were newcomers. Kids they were, kids who hadn't even begun to shave. He said as much to Charlie Draper, the coach, who sat as usual with one spiked shoe on the bench, his hand on his knee.

"They'll go," remarked Charlie. "You watch;

they'll vanish fast enough when you and Bob Russell and the varsity come back. Then we got us this guy Young."

"Young? Who is he?"

"Who is he? Haven't you heard about Lester Young? The rookie Mac paid almost twenty-five thousand dollars for, practically sight unseen, too?"

"Must be good."

"Good!" The coach ejected tobacco juice onto the grass twelve feet from the dugout's rim. "Roy, he ain't good. He's Superman."

Roy was interested. It was the first time he had ever heard Draper talk like this. Usually the coach was noncommittal about young ballplayers, for he had been around far too long to go out on a limb for a rookie, even the best of them. A great many things could happen in their development, he always said. So Roy sat up. "What position does he play, Charlie?"

"Dunno. Nobody knows. Why, that bird can play anywhere on a ballclub, and do anything. Roy, it looks as if we got ourselves another Babe Ruth. He hits the ball a country mile, he's a better than average fielder, fast as Man O'War, and they say he can pitch, too."

Roy sat back, thinking: Hope they don't put him in the outfield, what with me, and Swanny back from third again, and one or two boys like Alan Whitehouse and Paul Roth coming from the service. Then there's those two boys from Montreal. He sat there half-listening to the voices about him, to the shoptalk and chatter which was once so familiar that he really never heard it. Now it was almost foreign; it rang in his ears.

"Look at Steve up there," said someone along the bench. Roy didn't know the speaker. "He's got power, sure; and he's loose as ashes at the plate, but he won't lay off that low curve. See there . . . see that!"

"I know. It'll run him right out of this-here league."

"Know what? I told him that last night. I says to him: 'Kid, unless you lay off that low ball, you ain't gonna get anywhere but Birmingham.' I told him."

"Yeah. He thinks the only kind of a hit that goes in the batting average is a homer. Well, he won't be round next year when the boys come back."

Then a familiar figure sauntered across from the batting cage around the plate. Roy could hardly believe his eyes. For the man looked like Casey, the sports reporter, but this was a thinner, fitter Casey, tanned and lean. Here come the questions, Roy thought. However, he knew better how to parry questions, and he was sincerely interested in the change that had come over the newspaperman.

Casey, with his reporter's eye, spotted Roy on the bench immediately, and came up, hand out, genuinely glad to see him again. They exchanged greetings, and it appeared that Casey had been overseas as a war correspondent. To Roy, war correspondents were merely sportswriters in uniform. But Casey had seen service. He had been with the 4th Marines at Iwo Jima, had gone back to enter Manila with the 37th Division, had flown over Tokyo more than once. Roy's respect for him increased. The change in his appearance was quite understandable.

Presently their conversation shifted from battles to baseball.

"Looks like you're in good condition, Roy."

"To you, yes, Jim. To a ballplayer, no."

"Why not? What's the matter?"

"Why, Jim, far as baseball is concerned I'm just a baby again. I mean I feel as though I was a rookie once more and had to fight for a job. I've got to train and train hard to get my wind and legs in some sort of decent shape. That takes time, y'know."

Then someone yelled at him from above. Jack MacManus wanted to see him in the office. He went up to find the genial owner in a cordial and responsive mood. Asking casually about his condition, the boss explained that all returned servicemen on the club were given a physical examination by a specialist. After some more conversation, he took up the telephone and made a date for Roy to see the doctor the next morning.

The following day Roy sat in the waiting room of the doctor's office in the hospital, reading Casey's column. The sportswriter had wasted no time the previous afternoon.

Roy Tucker, ace center fielder of the Brooks, is home after four years in the Army, of which 22 months were spent abroad in Africa, Corsica and France. When drafted, back in '41, Roy was sent to Fort Riley to play on the ballteam there, but the usually good-natured farm boy made such a fuss they had to send him into combat duty overseas. He told them he didn't come into the Army to play baseball, and meant it, too. Finally they sent him across late in '42 as a sergeant in the 12th Airforce, where he had fifty-six missions over Europe, was brought down, captured, and escaped shortly before D-Day. The Kid from Tomkinsville refused to talk about his Army experiences, although he returned with the Silver Star and other decorations. He looks in first-class shape and is ready to rejoin the club.

Yeah? Says he! How does he know?

"The doctor will see you now."

Tossing the paper aside quickly, he went inside. The man at the desk wore a long, white coat. He was thin, bald, with blue eyes and a warming smile. Best of all, he was not interested in baseball or the Dodgers, and asked no questions about the players. His conversation and his actions were crisp and businesslike. Apparently he cared for his job and nothing else.

Roy yanked off his clothes, feeling confidence in the man. Without a word the doctor pointed to the table. Roy climbed up, and the doctor went right to his weak spot. Feeling along his hip and leg, he found the tenderness immediately, punching here and there, bringing little exclamations of pain from Roy's lips, just as the French doctor had done. Then he took a tape measure from his pocket and, stretching out both legs, measured them carefully several times.

"H'm . . . h'm . . . h'm." Nothing more.

Taking hold of the left leg, he lifted it with infinite care from the table. To Roy's amazement, the leg when extended upward would only rise a few inches before that pain began shooting up his hip. Then the doctor tried to move it outward. Again it hurt. Next he told him to stand and bend over to the floor. Once more Roy was astonished to discover how tight and stiff he was, how the looseness and suppleness had vanished from his back. This man knew his job.

"Get dressed now. I'm sending you downstairs to X ray for examinations."

Roy must have been half an hour on that table. They X-rayed him from every position and every angle. His hip, his back, his leg, his calf were taken, then re-taken. On his return upstairs, the doctor was busy and he had to wait. Finally he was ushered into the office, where the man sat in his swivel chair, tapping a ruler against his desk. He looked curiously at him.

"You're a professional baseball player, I understand."

"Yessir. Just out of service."

"H'm." Then for twenty minutes he asked Roy questions about his fall in France, about the crash of the plane, the angle at which it fell, the position he had been in, the tossing about that ensued. He took notes of everything, writing down each answer carefully. At last he swung round abruptly.

"Mr. Tucker . . ." He scratched his head.

Roy reflected that this was the first time he had been addressed that way for many years.

"Mr. Tucker, I haven't, of course, seen your X rays yet. But I believe they'll show that you threw your sacroiliac out of place in that plane crash in France, and that this has been causing pressure on your sciatic nerve. The sciatic nerve? That runs all the way down your leg from your hip, here. You evidently have a badly inflamed nerve condition in that left hip. You see, unconsciously you've been favoring your left side, which is why, as I suspected when I saw you walk in, your left leg is almost an inch shorter than your right."

"Shorter! Than my right one?"

"Yes, you see in the past year you've been continually favoring that side, and as a result your leg has actually shrunk nearly one inch. It's a common thing, very common. Don't worry. Now I believe, though as I say I have yet to see the plates, that we ought to give you an Ober."

"An Ober! What's that?"

He laughed, a friendly, reassuring laugh. "It's an operation named after a surgeon in Boston who invented it. We cut the muscles from here"—he placed his left hand on the top of Roy's left hip—"to here." The hand went diagonally across the hip. "That's done to release them, so you can swing out your leg. It was locked, you may have noticed, on the table. When do you think . . . it would be convenient?"

Boy! Well, if it's gotta come, it's gotta come. "Tomorrow."

The doctor laughed once more. "Not tomorrow. I'm afraid I'm busy all this week. How about next Thursday?"

It was nearing the season's end. This you instantly knew by the lack of pressure among the players, by the rows of empty seats in the boxes, by the turf, scarred and worn in the September sunshine. The batting cage was up around home plate, and the hitters were out there swinging freely at Fat Stuff's deliveries.

The batters rolled up to the plate, took their raps, one, two, three, and strolled slowly back to the dugout, thrusting their clubs into the batrack, pausing for a drink from the cooler before slumping upon the bench. Only one player on the field was nervous. Not because it was Roy Tucker Day in Flatbush, nor because the bleachers were jammed with yammering kids, and large signs hung from the balcony in center field saying:

WELCOME HOME, ROY

HULLO, KID

WELCOME BACK, TUCK

Roy was nervous because it was his first game of baseball, his first chance since his operation, and so much depended on it.

The sportswriters, who as a rule avoided a game with the Phils like an attack of cholera, were out in force. They surrounded him upon the bench, the inevitable Casey in the van, hammering him with questions of all sorts, about flying, about his injury, about his operation. He sat there tapping two bats against the dugout floor, brushing his cap back from his forehead.

"Yeah, I think the operation did me good. Anyhow I feel looser than I was last month. Who? Dr. Davison. He's supposed to be the best orthopedic surgeon in New York. Spell it? O-r-t . . . Shoot, that's your baby, Mac. How's that, Stanley? Why, yes, I do, really. I feel just like a rookie again. I realize there's some comers on this ballclub, and I've got to earn a job on the Dodgers same's I did seven years ago. No, sir, I'm not taking anything for granted."

[109]

The photographers swarmed around, clamoring as usual, so he stepped from the dugout and stood before them in the sunshine, holding the two bats in his hand, scowling slightly as he glanced down at the kneeling circle of cameramen, listening once more to their familiar appeals. "This way, Roy . . . This way, kid . . . Look over here, will ya please, Tuck . . . One more, Roy . . . Hey, Tuck, one more. Just one."

Finally he was permitted to sink back in peace upon the bench, and the sportswriters turned away for other prey. He sat listening to Casey telling Charlie Draper about an incident that had happened at the Yankee Stadium the previous afternoon. It concerned a war-time rookie who had gone to bat against Spud Chamberlain of the Yanks, just released from service. Casey related the yarn in his customary picturesque manner. "See now, Chuck, this youngster never heard of Spud. He was in high school in Little Rock when Chamberlain left to go into the Army. So when the old man comes in there along in the seventh, he gets two strikes on the kid, quick. Then he explodes his curve, you know, and bang! Mr. Rookie is on the bench, and the old maestro is laughing in his beard.

" 'Gee,' the kid says to Ed in the dugout. 'That's the best curve I've seen all season. Who is that pitcher, anyhow?' "

" 'Oh, just a pre-war ballplayer,' says Ed. 'Feller by the name of Chamberlain. That pre-war stuff is mighty potent, isn't it?' "

The coach nodded. "Yep, and he wasn't kidding, either. Well, the professionals have returned, and it's sure a pleasure to see some of these old-timers go to work on a batter nowadays. You take Fat Stuff, f'rinstance. When he gets a batter 2 and 2, he doesn't just wish the ball up. No, sir, he gets it in there with something on it, and good enough so the hitter can't afford to lay off, either."

The bell rang and the team took the field, or rather both teams took the field. They gathered round the plate, a moment of agony for Roy, while the gang in the bleachers rose cheering, giving him the warmest and throatiest of welcomes, glad to see him back and showing it, too. The president of the Borough stepped forward, a fine leather traveling case in his hand. Roy was so confused by it all he hardly could hear the words.

". . . Credit to our town and our team . . . fine

athlete and a fine soldier . . . welcome you home again . . ."

"Thank you, sir. Thanks very kindly; much obliged. Please thank all the boys; thank you very much indeed."

Then Swanny took the bag from his hand, the plate was cleared, and the game actually began. The Phils went down, and then after two men had flied out, the moment came that Roy had so often pictured, that he had dreamed about across half a world. He was putting on the batting cap with the plastic plate over his temples, taking the two bats from the boy, and chucking him the rosin bag again. Once more he was swinging up to the plate, stepping into the box for the first time in five long years. As he stood there, his bat in his hand, the kids in the bleachers rose with a thunderous and heartening roar. Shouts and whistles of encouragement came to him from the grandstands. Flatbush was celebrating the return of her favorite son.

He took the opening pitch; then swung on the second, a high, slow curve, the kind he usually liked. Somehow it didn't come off. He didn't seem to have it. He was stiff, failing utterly to get his shoulders behind the bat. The ball rolled gently toward first, and the baseman slapped it on him as he passed. The fans, who had risen with a roar as his bat swung, subsided with a disappointed moan.

The score was even at two apiece for most of the game, and then in the lower half of the seventh, the Phils got men on first and second. The next batter caught a fast ball on the nose, sending it on a line over the pitcher into the field. As he charged in from his old spot in center, Roy saw the familiar figure of Spike at short leap through the air, vainly lunging for the ball with his gloved hand. Rushing in, Roy realized the drive was dipping, and tried to get down to it, to bend over. Somehow he was tight, locked up, unable to get down. The ball went through his hands for a triple to the fence.

They came into the ninth with the Phils ahead, four to two. Spike, who never liked being beaten, and cared even less to be licked by a last-place club, walked up and down the bench calling for a hit. Swanny led off by working a pass. The next batter hit a grasscutter that sent Swanny to second, but was himself nabbed at first. Again Roy stepped to the plate, knocking the dirt from his spikes, this time determined to smack the ball. Out in center the kids were shrieking in unison: WE WANNA HIT.

WE WANNA HIT. WE WANNA HIT. He connected on the third pitch, but again he was stiff, unable to get any power behind his bat. The ball dribbled down the line, and he was an easy out. Discouraged at this weak and futile effort, he came back to the bench, shaking his head. I'm not right. Gosh, I'm not right yet!

Spike was on deck, however, with a clean single to right that scored Swanny. He stood on the bag, signaling for Lester Young to pinch hit for the next batter. Charlie Draper uncurled his legs as the big rookie swung up to the plate.

"This guy may unload one into the bleachers if that pitcher gets the least bit careless," he remarked.

The words were hardly out of his mouth when the rookie exploded the first pitch. You could tell it was soundly hit by the ring of bat and ball. It soared into the sky, high, high, and dropped in a mob scene of excited kids in the second tier of the stands in deep center field.

Back in the locker room ten minutes later, Roy stepped into the telephone booth before he had even showered. He dialed a number. "Give me Dr. Davison's office, please."

The next morning he was in the surgeon's office.

Again there was the same process, the same careful examination, the leg-lifting with the pain shooting up his hip, the slow, labored bending toward the floor, the measurements of each leg. The doctor stood there a minute, feeling Roy's hip, saying nothing. Then he examined the X rays with attention, and finally told Roy to dress.

"Mr. Tucker, we've got your leg fixed so far as the outward motion is concerned; but it's plain you are still getting that pressure on your nerve there." He looked at the pictures in his hand. Then he looked up, hesitated a minute, and said, "I think perhaps we'd better try a leg-stretching operation next."

Suddenly the horrible truth was apparent to Roy. He isn't sure. He doesn't know for certain what will cure me; he's experimenting.

Two months before he had assented eagerly to an operation, groping for any relief that was offered. Now it seemed harder. Was this the right thing? Would it really help? Would it cure him or at least put him on the road to being cured? His whole career depended on it, on this man and his skill.

He sat, unable to talk, unable to make a decision. Back in the Air Force he had wanted only one

[115]

thing—to be discharged as soon as possible, to be a civilian once more, to be back with the club. Once there, he had been sure all problems would soon be solved. Now he was slowly finding out that problems arose in civilian life as well, only here he must settle them. No one was telling him what to do now. Roy Tucker had to make the decisions for himself.

CHAPTER

14

AFTER the leg-stretching operation in December, Roy headed south. He reached Florida a month before the rest of the team, because he was anxious to get into condition for the season ahead. There was lots to be done. Beyond question the last operation had helped. It had definitely removed some of the pressure from his hip and leg, made him looser. The rest, he felt sure, was exercise.

So he reached Florida early and began working hard on conditioning his legs. If your legs are right, your timing is right, and everything else is easy. He had noticed some of the returning veterans try to play ball the previous summer, and they looked to him as if they had lead in their shoes. It proved how far he had to go. By this time his stiffness, his trick of favoring that left side, had almost become an unconscious habit. He had often heard that if you start out with a bad habit in the spring, you're licked, because you'll keep it all season. The time for a player to get rid of a bad habit is in spring training season, not after the campaign has begun.

Slowly the crowd arrived. Spike Russell with Jack MacManus and the coaches came first, and the others checked in every day. Bob Russell came back from the Navy, and Jocko Klein, just discharged from the Army, returned also. Swanny, as usual, was a hold-out. He invariably was in the spring, hoping, by this device, to escape a few days of the grueling early-season training. There were three or four rookies trying for each position. Many of the pitching staff Roy knew before the war had vanished; some traded, some dropped out of the game, some gone back to the minors as scouts or managers of farm clubs. Only Bones Hathaway, Raz Nugent, and Fat Stuff remained. In place of the others was a crowd of youngsters from Montreal, Savannah, and Olean, boys with poise and promise. Roy watched them carefully. Notwithstanding the constant warnings of the coaches, they were like a bunch of colts, almost burning the catcher's hands off during the first few days. Regretting it, too, when sore arms developed like an epidemic a short while afterward.

Roy knew he would find the going rough. Players who were tolerated in the war years because there was no one else, were quickly thrown aside; newcomers were sifted out with dispatch and released or sent to the farms. Sometimes he felt confident of getting the stiffness out of his sore left leg. The warm Florida sunshine helped; so did the daily massage, and occasionally he would have spurts of his old-time speed and bursts of his former power. Other days he would find himself tied up, lame and helpless.

In the initial practice game between the varsity and the scrubs, he got a hit the first time up. Then in the fourth, with the bases loaded, he popped up weakly to the shortstop. So he went back to the dugout, kicking the bats in disgust, and slumping disconsolately on the bench. Spike Russell stepped over from the coaching lines behind third and called to the bench.

"O. K. there, Roy. Take your shower, boy, and get yourself a good rub-down. Lester, go in at center, will ya?"

Roy rose and slouched to the clubhouse in left, discouraged and unhappy. As he passed, Spike came over, putting an arm round his shoulder and walking a little way out with him. "Roy, take it easy, take it easy. You're pressing. You hit a bad ball that time. Say, you were all tightened up; you're worrying. Don't worry, boy; I got confidence in you. Remember, you've been away from the game a long, long time. Just don't lose confidence in yourself, that's all."

It was extremely hard not to lose confidence in oneself. It was difficult to keep plugging when you saw those youngsters cavorting round you, spearing liners back by the fence, smacking pitches over the scoreboard in deep left field. At this time Roy's old friends helped, especially Spike and Fat Stuff and Raz Nugent. Raz had great affection for Roy and did his best to cheer him up. If he found the Kid moping in his room, he would yank him away to the pictures or take him outdoors for a walk. One night he insisted on taking Roy on what he termed a secret mission. They finally crashed a high school dance where Raz ended as a soloist with the orchestra, and became the sensation of the evening.

"That big guy slays me," remarked Spike the next morning when he heard about the episode. "Remember in Chicago how he scared Red Allen to death couple of years ago?" said Charlie Draper. "Remember, Red was rooming with him, and one day he comes in to find a suicide note on the bureau. 'Life is too much for me,' it says. Red looks at the open window, and just then Raz yanks himself up over the window sill where he's been hanging ten stories above the ground. Anything for a laugh, that guy."

The big pitcher could invariably be called on for amusement whenever things became grim. One of the rookies had a habit of picking up newspapers from the seats in hotel lobbies, and Raz caught him sneaking the sports section from under the arm of a teammate one afternoon. The following morning when he reached the clubhouse, the newcomer found his locker completely stuffed with ancient and excessively dirty newspapers.

Raz's chief pleasure, however, was catching the youngsters on the hidden ball trick, an act in which he was aided and abetted by Bob Russell. Thanks to Razzle's clever acting and Bob's amazing quickness of foot and hand, one rookie after another had to trot back to the bench from second in chagrin.

On a close play at second, Raz would come storming over and pretend to take the ball from Bob. On his way back toward the mound, he would whirl around, apparently all set to throw the ball to Bob in the hope of catching the rookie off the bag. Standing just back of the mound, he would pretend to shake off his catcher, while the unsuspecting runner took a lead. At which point Bob Russell, who had been holding the ball the whole time, would charge over and tag him.

Raz never worked the trick often. He usually saved it for the tight moment of a tight game. Sometimes the coaches knew what was coming and helped him to let the lesson sink in, but in any case he was unusually efficient in snaring the unwary.

Once in a close practice game a rookie first baseman, who had been one of Raz's victims, tried to return the compliment. Razzle had made his first and almost his only base hit of their Florida stay, and came triumphantly to first. It was in the ninth, with the score tied, and he represented the winning run. In the box the pitcher went through various motions, picking up the rosin bag, tossing it carelessly to the ground. Then, standing off the rubber, he assumed his pitching pose, watching first base

over one shoulder. Raz, however, remained anchored on the sack. At last he turned to the rookie
beside him with scorn.

"You young busher, don't you know Raz Nugent
invented that play?"

CHAPTER

15

Roy sat alone in his hotel room reading the local afternoon newspaper which he had just purchased downstairs in the lobby. Flipping it open to the sports pages, he was suddenly attacked by a most unpleasant feeling.

Better count Roy Tucker out. With Swanson's arrival in camp, Spike Russell has benched him temporarily. Besides being in a batting slump, Roy apparently has not as yet fully recovered from his army injury. It could be that the Brooks will be obliged to go through the season without their ace gardener; but judging by the first few weeks of practice here, it looks as if Lester Young will make the boys in the center field stands at Ebbets Field forget the Kid from Tomkinsville ever existed. Les will bat almost as well, will field better, and steal more bases in a month than Roy would in a year.

Count Roy Tucker out! He threw the newspaper across the room. Steal more bases in a month than I will in a year, hey! What a laugh! Now he knows that's not true. Why does he say those things? They're all the same, these guys, anything for an angle.

Then he began to think back a little; to recall incidents that were unimportant at the time, but might add up to something; Casey's brief greeting the other day as he turned toward Young beside the batting cage; the newspapermen surrounding the rookie in the lockers every day after practice; the daily stories about him, his photographs spearing liners in the field, sliding into second, or batting against Raz. It did add up to something, and that something was not reassuring.

Roy rose in annoyance, his aching hip angry and protesting at the sudden movement. It seemed to be acting up worse of late. Slowly he walked across the room, stooping to pick up the newspaper on the floor. His position was exactly opposite the full-length mirror on the door of the bathroom, and suddenly he saw himself for the first time. Not Roy Tucker. Not the speediest man in the National League. But an ancient gent with an expression of pain upon his face, unable to stoop, bending over awkwardly toward the floor with a stiffness dreadful to behold.

Once again he leaned over and tried to pick up that newspaper, watching the mirror closely as he did so. Then he turned and sat down on the bed, trembling. The discouragement, this mind struggling in a body that was incapable of responding, seemed more than he could bear. He felt suddenly nearer the breaking point than any time since Fried Spratt had crashed in France.

Now he could feel their pity and understand it. No wonder! No wonder Casey and the boys all let me alone. Good grief, they see me as I am. This is how I look to other folks. For the first time he saw himself as he was, for the first time appreciated the extent of his physical handicap. He sat on the edge of the bed, quite unable to move for a long time, thinking.

Why, that's how I seem, that's the way I must look to the sportswriters and the other boys on the club. For the first time he realized what they must be saying about him. Poor old Tuck! There's a guy trying to do something he isn't fit for. They were all watching his struggle, anxious to help. Yet anxious also to say: "Brother, you can't do it. Why not pack up?"

Roy hardly slept at all that night. Either the shock reacted in some way upon the angry nerve in his leg, or else it was getting worse, and rapidly. His hip ached steadily, so intensely that sleep was quite out of the question. Long before light entered the room, he had decided to go north immediately and get fixed up once and for all. As dawn broke, the pain up and down his leg was more than he could endure. Trying to get some aspirin from the bathroom, he discovered that he was unable to put his foot to the ground, and it was necessary to hop across the room on one foot like a cripple. Once he was in bed again, his tortured tossing woke Swanny, his roommate. At seven Swanny got worried and insisted on calling the house physician, who arrived half an hour later. By then, Roy was actually writhing in agony on the floor, with Spike Russell and Swanny trying vainly to do something to help him.

The doctor took one quick look, felt the leg gingerly, asked a few curt questions and then, stepping to the telephone, called the local hospital for an ambulance. The three men tried to dress him. It hurt too much, so they pulled his bathrobe over

[127]

his pajamas and rolled him in a couple of blankets, groaning and protesting. The weight of the blankets, the slightest touch on his leg, sent spasms of pain up and down the nerve. When the stretcher came, it took the three men and two orderlies ten minutes to get him upon it. Then they took him downstairs in the freight elevator.

Through the veil of suffering which engulfed him, he saw the scared faces of his teammates in the halls, felt the agonizing jolting as they lifted him from the elevator and carried him along a corridor, out to the street where a small crowd had collected around the waiting ambulance. They slid the stretcher onto the racks, and rolled through the quietness of early morning to the Fisher Memorial Hospital.

Roy Tucker did not put his foot to the ground for over a month.

16

LIKE the world of France and the Gestapo, this was another and different world. All thought of the outdoors and baseball was as far away as the Army and Europe. Every bit of Roy's effort and attention in that lonely hospital room was upon one thing: pain, enduring it, alleviating it, conquering it. The job before him was to conquer pain; the sooner he could start the struggle the better. The first day the doctor gave him some dope to permit sleep. Yet always, however he lay and whatever way he turned, pain was in the background.

"I'm going to try ultraviolet rays on your leg," said the doctor. "Had some unusually good luck with it on several patients, and it certainly can't do you any harm. Suppose you start with two minutes —that's if you can stand it. Two minutes on your hip, your thigh, and then have it moved down to the calf of your leg. Nurse, I'd like you to get that lamp up the first thing tomorrow morning, please."

So twice every day they wheeled the lamp into his room, twice daily the nurse stood timing him, turning the heat on his thigh, and moving it down to his calf at the end of two minutes. Far from stopping the pain, the lamp seemed to intensify it. At first he felt the agony was impossible to stand. And the treatment seemed to have no effect whatever on the constant ache he suffered during the remainder of the day. Then about the fourth morning he noticed that while the lamp was on, the pain was less intense, at least it did not start until after the first minute.

Progress. That was all he groped for, progress, progress of any sort, anything to show he was not going back. If only he could see some advance, if only he was sure he was not going backward, he felt he could endure the pain. He was told to increase the heat to three minutes on each spot. Under that burning torture from the lamp, it was necessary to lie with tight lips, clutching the steel bars at the head of the hospital bed, to summon all his strength and resolution to last out the daily ordeal. But the fact that he could endure it gave him confidence, a deep-seated something no pain could rock. He was determined to come back, he willed to come back, he knew he would, he must come back. In what way, he had no idea, but some way, somehow.

A sick athlete is a forgotten athlete, especially in professional sport. Only a short time before Roy had been news: a war veteran returned to the game, and therefore in the headlines. Now things were different. In this new world he was left alone. Here he was merely an occasional odd item at the bottom of some sportswriter's daily file. "Roy Tucker continues to make slow progress in the Fisher Memorial Hospital here in town . . . Les Young had three for three in the practice game against the Reds in Tampa this afternoon . . . Two aspiring rookies showed up in camp today."

Roy never read the sports pages now. Baseball had no interest for him. All that was in the other world, the world which no longer existed. To think about returning to the team was too fantastic, too far away even to consider; his energy and efforts were needed for something far more important—progress. First he had to learn to sit up in bed, little by little, slowly and painfully. A minute, a minute and a half, two minutes, then he would slump down again, the pain forcing sweat out upon his forehead. The dose of the lamp gradually increased, and the doctor, who said nothing and promised nothing, nodded with approval at each visit in the morning.

Only a few of his old friends on the club bothered to drop in and see him: Swanny and Fat Stuff and Spike Russell. Once Bones Hathaway, the star pitcher just out of the service, came in. Roy was pleased and touched. MacManus sent him a huge bunch of flowers and every week a large basket of fruit, but stayed away himself. So March passed, the sun grew warmer, and the final games of the Grape-fruit League were held in Florida, as the teams prepared to journey north, playing each other in exhibition matches en route.

The last day of March was a big day for Roy. He sat up in a chair for the first time, only four minutes to be sure, but long enough to gobble a hasty lunch. This triumph was not accomplished without suffering; it left him gasping in pain on the bed afterward. Yet it was progress that could be seen, measured, which was all he asked. The pain he accepted. At least he was not going backward. Each morning the lamp was wheeled in. Baring his leg, he would turn over on his stomach and lie holding tightly to the bars at the head of the bed.

"Think you can stand it today? Can you take that extra minute this morning?" asked the nurse, watching his fists clench on the bars of the bedstead.

"Sure I can take it. Go on."

Once he had wondered whether, if the Gestapo had tried anything, he could have endured physical torture. Now he knew.

In this different world he found it was necessary to learn to walk all over again. He was a baby and walking was a difficult, almost impossible task. At first he would hop to the bathroom on his good leg, then gradually the left foot came gently to the ground, one step today, two steps tomorrow, three steps the next day before that agonizing pain started creeping up his leg and thigh. And every morning the lamp, for fifteen minutes now, on leg, hip, and calf. It was the doctor one morning who noticed the steel bars at the head of the bed bent inward where in his agony under the intense heat of the lamp Roy had held to them.

By the middle of April, he was able and anxious to go north. The trip by car to Jacksonville and by plane to New York was exhausting, and sent him to bed on his arrival at the hotel where the club stayed. There he remained for several days recuperating, until at last he was able to hobble down to a taxi and so to the hospital to Dr. Davison's office.

The surgeon in his long white coat sat listening intently to Roy's story. He was concentrating on everything said, asked few questions, simply nodded occasionally, a frown on his forehead, his hands clasped, thinking. Then he rose. "Come into the next room."

Again Roy lay on the now familiar table while the doctor examined him carefully. "I was afraid of this . . . yes . . . sore there? It is . . . h'm . . . and the hip too, here?" For a long while he went over his back, lifted his leg ever so gently. Then gravely he said: "All right. You can dress now."

Roy dressed and hobbled back into the surgeon's office, despair in his heart. Is this the end? Am I washed up? Am I through with baseball?

The surgeon looked straight at him. Bad news. Roy felt it in every gesture, in his glance, in his warm and sympathetic movement as he placed one hand lightly on his knee.

"Mr. Tucker, yours is an aggravated case, and I

hardly know what to say. I can fix you up for ordinary daily life, but unfortunately you're an athlete, which is quite different. It might be that after some more rest, after the inflammation in that nerve has subsided, another leg-stretching operation would help. But I wouldn't be sure, I wouldn't promise . . ." He leaned back, his hands behind his head, looking at the ceiling now.

"You wouldn't promise to cure me?"

The doctor nodded. There was silence, and the traffic noise far below came through the open window. Then this *is* the end. The end of it all, the finish. I'm through with baseball. "You mean I wouldn't be any better after another operation than I was when I went south this spring?"

Again the doctor nodded. Then he rose. His hand went out, and his long thin fingers yanked nervously at the window shade. "Frankly, I've done about everything I honestly feel I can for you. There's nothing more I would suggest at present." He walked across the room. "Except one thing. This is only a suggestion, and you may not wish to follow it. There's an Austrian doctor over here now, a Dr. Rittenbusch. He is called a bloodless surgeon; he works by manipulation. He studied under Lorenz, the famous Viennese, and escaped during the war. I'm told he had some amazing success with baseball players recently."

"What players?" Roy's heart leaped, and through the film of despair came a ray of hope. "What players?"

"I can't quite recall their names—one pitcher who, I think, was troubled with bursitis. And then a friend of mine sent him a case much like yours, a boy named . . . Tonelli, I think it was."

"You don't mean Ray Tonelli, the second baseman of the Giants, do you?"

"Yes, that's the one. He had the same trouble as yours, and nearly every doctor here in town had given up on the case. A bad sciatic condition . . ."

"I'll see him," said Roy, interrupting.

The surgeon pressed a button. "Miss Gallagher, get me Dr. Rittenbusch's address. No, hold on a minute; I'd like to talk to him. Get him for me on the telephone. He lives somewhere outside the city, I think."

So, on the day the Brooks opened the season in Boston, Roy journeyed to Mount Vernon to see Dr. Rittenbusch. Without much hope, either.

CHAPTER

17

———————

THE house in the suburbs was a small, unpretentious
dwelling with a tiny waiting room and office attached to one side. Roy's heart, buoyed by hope,
sank as he saw it. After the hospitals and waiting
rooms and glistening doctor's offices he had seen in
his long journey through pain, this place was unim-
pressive and disappointing. The doctor himself came
briskly from within, and led him inside. The work-
room contained a desk, a filing cabinet, the long,
high table to which Roy was now so accustomed,
and nothing else.

There were surprises in store. For one thing, the
doctor was impressive by the confidence he had in
himself. He was a man with graying hair, huge
shoulders, a big torso, and a slim waist. Whatever
his age, he was an advertisement for himself.

"Now then." He sat at his desk, beaming through horn-rimmed glasses. "You are Mr. . . . Mr. . . .?"

"Tucker. Roy Tucker."

He nodded. "So, so. How did your injury occur, please?" He leaned over, attentive.

For perhaps the sixtieth time Roy explained briefly the crash in France, the ensuing pain, the operations, the crack-up in Florida. The old chap sat listening with attention, quite evidently concentrating, nodding yet saying not a word. Finally he twisted his lips together. "Ah, I see. Now, will you please sit here on the edge of this table. So."

"Take my clothes off?"

"Not necessary. Just your jacket." He walked with quick, short steps around the table, and began running his fingers ever so gently up and down Roy's spine, slowly probing. "H'm . . . h'm . . . so . . . I see . . . ah . . . there . . . ah, so . . . no wonder you suffer . . . how long did you say you have this?" Those fingers were moving skillfully up and down the Kid's backbone, yet curiously causing him no pain whatever. There was a frown on the face of the doctor as he worked.

"Almost two years now."

"So! Yes, I see. Now please, lie down flat, on

[138]

your back." For a minute or two he continued to feel along his backbone, up and down. Then he straightened up. "That's all."

Roy sat up. "You mean that's all? All for today?"

"Yes. Your nerve is still too inflamed for me to treat you now. Next week, perhaps."

"Well, do you think . . . Can you help me any? Get me on my feet again?" By now Roy hated the word cure quite as much as most doctors did. He was somewhat disappointed by the man's actions.

"I think I can. You're young yet. Last fall I have a case even worse than yours, some other baseball player. Let me see, what *was* that chap's name?"

"You don't maybe mean Ray Tonelli of the Giants, do you?"

A warm smile brightened the doctor's face. "That's it. Tonelli."

Roy smiled also. Imagine forgetting Tonelli, the leading Giant hitter, the man who always batted in more runs than anyone in either league. Names, he later discovered, meant nothing whatever to this amazing character.

"Yes, I fix him up, get him back playing, and he was in a worse condition than you are at present. There is a partial dislocation of the hip and the sacrum, like this, so, and that dislocation is the base of your trouble."

It meant nothing to Roy, nothing save for one sentence. "You say mine isn't as bad as Ray Tonelli's?"

"Goodness no, nothing like. Yours hadn't gone as far as his. I believe I can straighten you out in time. You see that bone there is partially dislocated; it's pressing on a nerve and naturally causing you pain. Now let's see, how about Tuesday, that's a week from tomorrow? If you rest carefully, take things easy, some of the inflammation should be gone from that nerve and I think I can treat you then."

"Tuesday next, that's the 25th, isn't it? What time?"

He consulted an appointment book. Roy observed that it was completely full for the following week. Whatever else the man needed, he certainly didn't need new patients.

"Let's see now, say ten in the morning. All right, then, Tuesday next, at ten."

Roy climbed clumsily into the parked taxi at the curb. A funny old geezer. Looks as if he knew what he was about. But imagine anyone forgetting Ray Tonelli of the Giants.

CHAPTER

18

———————————————

"Now then. Lie down, please. H'm . . . h'm . . . there. I think I can do something today." The doctor's big hands were moving up and down Roy's spine as he leaned over. "Yes. I think I can . . . today . . . do something." There was a moment's silence. "There!"

He uttered a little grunt, at the same time giving Roy's back a hug, a sort of tight squeeze, a gentle squeeze that was perceptible and nothing more. What Roy did feel was an immediate relaxation of the tightness up and down his spine. The pressure was disappearing, the pain also.

"There! Good, so far. I've put that sacroiliac of yours back in place. Now the thing to do is to keep it there. Oh, anyone can put it back—that's simple." His fingers like spiders roved up and down the back, so gently that Roy could hardly feel them, yet always loosening, relieving the pressure. He talked as he worked. "That articulation there . . . between the hip and the sacrum. I had a case like yours only last year, a baseball player he was, too . . . boy by the name of . . . by the name of . . ." He paused, straightened up, the frown on his face.

Roy glanced up sharply at the earnest, wrinkled face, at the blue eyes behind the horn-rimmed glasses. Was he kidding? Not at all. The puzzled expression was honest and direct.

"Couldn't be Ray Tonelli of the Giants, could it?"

"Of course! You told me his name when you were in here ten days ago, didn't you? It took time to straighten that lad out."

With difficulty Roy kept silent. If it took time for Ray, how long would it take for himself? This was the 25th of April. Roy had learned the hard way that doctors never enjoy committing themselves on a patient's recovery, and seldom do. So he said nothing.

The big hands, the powerful thumbs were working underneath his body now, running a tattoo along his spine, easing the pressure. All the while he conversed in a kind of monologue.

"You had pain all up and down your left side and your left leg, didn't you? Yes, well, consequently you favored it, you leaned toward your right, you overworked your right side and neglected the muscles all up and down your left side, through here. They became soft through disuse. Now we must build these up again in order to regain normal equilibrium."

"But how?"

"Partly by treatment, first; but mostly by exercise."

"Exercise! You mean I can cure myself by exercise?"

"Certainly. If you do them faithfully."

"Doc, I'll walk on my head up and down Broadway if it'll get me back on that ballclub. You see, I've been around quite some time, and I never ducked anything yet." Hope surged up within him; for the first moment in long months his spirit rose.

The doctor straightened up, smiling. "Good. This is the stage when you must fight, when you can help yourself by fighting. If you will, you are cured." Now he was working again on the hip, going down the leg, kneading the calf with the softest of touches, then suddenly unfastening the shoe.

"My foot's O.K., Doc."

The big man paid no attention, yanked off the shoe and removed the stocking. "Yes . . . h'm . . . you never get a hip out of place that you don't affect the muscles and the ligaments. These you have to correct by working on the foot." He was massaging the instep, then pulling and working on the bones round the toes, always gently, always slowly, and always competently. The stocking and shoe were replaced, and he got after the other foot. Again he replaced sock and shoe when finished.

"There! That about does it for today. I shall want to see you . . . let's see . . . about Friday. Suppose we say Friday next, at the same time. Then perhaps twice next week, and maybe once more; maybe not. After that it's up to you."

"You mean the exercises?"

"Yes, let me show you now." With the agility of a youngster, he flipped himself over on the table, upon his back, his hands flat along the surface.

"Only three of them; but you must do them correctly or they are of no value, and you must do them regularly, twice a day."

Roy stood erect and comfortable for almost the first time since Fried Spratt came down upon the tiny airfield in the Dordogne. "You don't need to worry about that. If I say I will, I will."

"So, good. Now, here is the first one." Carefully the doctor explained the exercises to Roy, demonstrating each one in slow motion, repeating them until he was certain he understood.

"D'you think, doctor, I might . . . maybe get back in there before the end of the summer?"

"It depends on you. You can run; you'll probably be able to run as fast as you ever did in two months. But if you make sudden jerks or starts, you're likely to throw that back of yours out again."

"Then we start from the beginning?"

"That's right. Watch yourself carefully; above all no sudden movements. And do those exercises."

Roy stepped into the taxi. Bending over had ceased to be the incredible agony it formerly had been, and he got in almost with ease.

Will I take those exercises! Will I! If I'm not a fighter, I'm nothing.

CHAPTER

19

THERE were times when the loud-voiced president of the club bothered Roy; but Jack MacManus had one quality that endeared him to every man on the team—loyalty. If a man tried and tried hard, he was for him. He was especially loyal to those who had helped him win pennants. Some club owners might have released Roy outright, or at any rate taken him off the active list. As he sat in the boss's outer office waiting for their first conference since his crackup, Roy had no fear of either event happening.

From within could be heard the booming voice of the big executive, and softer tones which Roy recognized as the voice of the pitcher, Bones Hatha-way. Roy immediately guessed Bones was getting a call-down. Although MacManus had great loyalty for the players, if he felt one of them was not trying, he jumped him immediately. The fact was that the big pitcher had been in and out all spring. When the team left for their western trip two days previously, he had been kept in Brooklyn.

All this Roy knew. He did not, however, anticipate the sentence he heard from the adjoining room.

"So there you are! I don't know whether you'll be back or not. That's entirely up to you, my boy, strictly up to you, as it is to everyone on this club. Truth is, you're plain lazy. You're trying to coast along on your reputation, and you just can't do that in this post-war baseball. And you've developed one bad fault. You're unable—or else you are afraid—to hit that strike zone with your first two pitches any more. Consequently you are behind the batter and always in trouble. I can't tell whether you can correct this in Montreal or not. It's up to you."

Montreal! Sending Bones to Montreal. Say, that's tough, that's exile, that is.

"No pitcher can be behind the hitters and win. Bones, look, I believe in you. I know you have the stuff. I have faith in you or I'd give you an outright release here this morning. But whether we pick up your option depends entirely on you."

There was a pause in his lecture, as the pitcher

[147]

answered in despondent tones that Roy was unable to hear. Montreal! This must hurt. It's hard on a man's pride to be sent to the minors after three seasons in the big time, one on a championship club. To be going up river after three years in a Dodger uniform, with a one-way ticket in your pocket, isn't funny.

Suddenly the similarity of their situations came to him. Bonesey must come back the hard way, just as I must do. He's got to work things out for himself, same as I have, to prove himself all over again. And it won't be so easy for either of us, with these kids coming along.

Then the door burst open, and a red-faced Hathaway flew out of the president's sanctum. He was so agitated that he never even noticed Roy sitting quietly on a chair at one side.

"Come in, Roy, come right in, boy!" The handshake of the boss was warm and sincere. He glanced up under his thick eyebrows. "Got good news for me this morning?"

"Why, yes, sir. Yes, Mr. Mac, believe I have . . . at least I hope so. The doc thinks, he says now . . ."

The secretary was handing MacManus three or four letters, and he stood there reading them, issuing dictates, returning the letters to her, one by one; all the time paying not the slightest attention to his visitor, who slowed up, hesitated, stopped talking.

"Sit down, boy, sit down. Now tell me all about it. This man seems to have done you some good, doesn't he?"

Roy would have liked nothing better than to talk about his doctor; but it was difficult. The phone clicked gently every few seconds, and often the secretary entered and laid a memorandum, or the name of some caller waiting outside, upon the desk before the president's gaze. Only two things resulted definitely from the interview. One was that the boss still had faith in his ultimate recovery and still considered him a member of the club. The second was that he had arranged for Roy to work out each morning with the Yankees while the Dodgers were on their western trip, if he were well enough to try it.

Roy had finished his six treatments with Dr. Rittenbusch, and had been doing those exercises daily for weeks. The pain was gone, and he felt looser and freer in his movements from day to day, yet he dared put no pressure upon his leg. Indeed he was afraid to do so, because too much depended upon it. After a check-up in mid-June, the doctor told him he was ready to start training again if he would work into it gradually. He noticed Roy's hesitation.

"See here now. This is where you must learn to help yourself. There's nothing wrong with your leg now, but you're afraid to use it. You've got to get over that. If you believe in yourself, I'm convinced you can do anything. It's a problem of faith. This is something you must work out for yourself."

So Roy began, gingerly, tenderly, each morning at the Yankee Stadium. At first just a gentle jog around the field; then after several days two laps, and next three laps, faster still. Ever so slowly his confidence returned. In a week he found himself shagging flies, yet all the while half expecting that agony to return. The pain had become too much a part of him to put aside easily. But he kept at it, meanwhile going through the doctor's exercises twice each day with a fervor that was almost religious.

I'm gonna come back . . . I'm determined to come back . . . I *will* get back on that club again.

Each day he went a little further and did a little more, each day watching anxiously for the advent of those first spasms of pain. His speed returned, and only in his stopping and starting motions, the jerky movements, did he find himself slowed up. That, he realized, was mostly due to fear. Little by little he found himself thinking less of his handicap and more of that ball soaring toward him through the sky. One day he discovered himself racing hard for a deep drive, sweat pouring from his face. It was a wonderful, a happy fortnight. It also helped one afternoon when he stayed round for the opening game of a double-header, to see Ray Tonelli hopping about on second base like a rookie.

Finally the Brooks returned in triumph from their safari in the west, leading the league by nine games. The boys were affable and pleasant, genuinely glad to see Roy, even though Lester Young, as predicted, was tearing up the basepaths and starring in the Kid's old spot in center field. But everyone welcomed him back: his old friends, Fat Stuff and noisy Raz and Bob Russell and quiet Jocko Klein; also the rookies, Elmer Shiells, who was doing such a fine job at the hot corner, and the new pitchers—Mike Mehaffey and Eddie Stone and Jerry Fielding.

That first afternoon, Lester Young, big, powerful,

sure of himself, strode up to the dugout where Roy
was sitting.

"Glad to have you back again, Roy. How you
making it?"

The Kid looked at him quickly. Yes, he meant it.
Roy, who had disliked him at first, was disarmed.
"Shucks, I'm coming along, I guess, Lester. But it
looks to me like you boys out there are doing O.K.
without me."

The slugging outfielder went over to the batrack
and yanked out his war-club. Striding to the plate,
he called back over one shoulder: "You wait. We'll
need you plenty before this summer's over."

Yes, it was great to be back, to wear that old 34
again, to haul on the blue socks with the white
undersocks showing beneath, and the flannel shirt
with the word "Dodgers" across the front, and the
trousers patched over the hips where rival spikes
had gashed them, and the blue cap with the dirty-
white "B" on it. To step once more into the batter's
box, to feel his spikes dig into the thick turf of the
outfield, or just to sit there in the dugout watching
the splotched stands, the blue and white patches of
shirts, the dimness of the rows of seats in the upper

tier. It was great to be again in that familiar atmosphere and hear the talk.

"Looka that! See that stop!" Charlie Draper's
tones sounded over the bench. "Yes, sir, the professionals are back. As Raz put it, during the war a
pitcher stood out there and listened to the base
hits ringing past his nut. Now he looks up to see a
double-play on the same sort of ball."

Then from the other end Roy heard Casey's
tones, needling, trying as usual to get information
from Spike Russell, their fighting manager. Canny
Spike was too much for the clever sportswriter, although they fenced each other verbally each time
they met.

"But suppose he does, even if he does," persisted
Casey, "where you gonna use him?" This made Roy
sit up. They're talking about me. "Swanny's better'n
ever he was," Casey went on. "Paul Roth is batting
third in the league. As for Young, well, you would-
n't bench him for DiMag, would you?"

Then came Spike's tones and words that helped:
"A good ballplayer is a good ballplayer and a manager can't have too many of them. You can always
use them, and I'm stringing along with him." His
voice had decision and finality. The sentences and

the confidence that clung to them were like a pat on the back.

There, that's the sort of manager to have, that's the kind of guy to work for. I'm not quitting on this thing. It may take time, it may take all summer, but I'm coming back to this club.

Count Roy Tucker out! Lemme see, who was it said that?

CHAPTER

20

NINE games ahead the middle of July, that's really all right. Especially with the other teams back in the ruck, cutting each other's throats for you every day in the week. To stay on top, the Dodgers had to win the hard ones under the arc lights of the west. Those were the games they took. So back to Brooklyn, loose, easy, and confident. It was a good ballclub for Roy to return to, and this was the best return of all. Now he could almost see the end of his long, uphill climb.

Sitting on the bench in the dugout with its wide floorboards cut by the scraping and scuffing of thousands of spikes, Roy thought, I'd rather warm the bench for Spike Russell than be a regular on the Yanks. But I'm not going to be a bench-warmer all season. I'm determined to come back; I will get back on that club.

He sat listening to the crack of bat against ball, the thud of the catchers' mitts as the hurlers took their warm-ups, the friendly voices around, the shouts from the stands, the cries of the scorecard men, of old Jake Schultz especially. No one could mistake his tones.

The old fellow drew nearer. "Peanuts, they're ten a bag. Fresh roasted peanuts, they're ten a bag. Who's next up there? Getcha fresh roasted . . . fresh roasted . . . who's next? Why, Roy! Hullo there, glad to see you back, son."

"Hullo yourself, Jake. Mighty glad to be back. How's tricks?"

"Just fine, boy. How are you?"

"Me? I'm coming along. Business good this year, Jake?" It was no secret that he was the plutocrat of Ebbets Field. Never reticent regarding his earnings, Jake confessed to clearing from thirty to forty dollars a day on scorecards alone. He received a penny on each card and each bag of peanuts sold. His big money came from peanuts, and he had a system of his own in selling them.

"See now, I'm a psychologist. I don't chuck the

bags any old way. I throw 'em hard, with a flip, Roy, like this . . . see? And some wise guy with a girl, some show-off, he hollers and holds out his mitt. So I let him have it, hard as I can. He catches it and comes back for another. Slick, see? Yes, sir, business is good. You can't lose with a winning club; you can't help making dough. Well, kid, take care of yourself. We'll need you out there afore September." He passed on, his strong tones resounding over the hubbub. "Who's next? Fresh roasted . . . they're ten cents a bag . . . getcha fresh roasted."

Now that's the second person who has said that. Roy was only vaguely aware of the music from the organ above. Suddenly he really heard it. *"Take me out to the ballgame . . ."*

Then the hot haze of that summer morning on the big *Queen* came back to him—the bands on the pier and the guys aboard yelling at the Red Cross girls. *"For it's one . . . two . . . three strikes, you're out . . . at . . ."* No, sir, I'm not out. I'm back. They'll need me before September, and I'm gonna get my spot back on this club once more if it kills me.

The bell rang and the game commenced. It was a long game and a tough one, a pitcher's battle, with Eddie Stone, the young ace of the Brooks, against Earl Wingate, the Cub star. It was one of those dingdong affairs in which the pitchers hand-cuffed the batters, and the great crowd was tense and restless all afternoon as neither side could get a run. Inning after inning saw only goose eggs on the scoreboard in right. When you have hurlers in the box with perfect control and two clubs playing errorless baseball, you have a stalemate. Lester Young had a couple of chances to bring home that important run, but was unable to get the ball out of the infield. Other hitters were just as bad. So they came into the tenth, the eleventh, the twelfth, and the thirteenth, with lots of cold suppers waiting for their owners around Flatbush.

As the Dodger pitcher slumped down on the bench at the end of the Cub's thirteenth, Roy noticed his heavy breathing. Quite obviously tired; Spike will go for someone else. Yet although a pinch-hitter was indicated, for he was lead-off man that inning, Spike's voice down the bench startled Roy.

"Go on out there, Tuck, and get us a hit."

Roy didn't move for a moment. Well, here goes! Will I stiffen up again? Will that leg tighten up the way it did before?

He rose, stepped outside to the batrack, picked up the lumber, cracked the two bats together, and tossed one aside. As he walked out, a shriek from the stands drowned out the voice of the announcer.

"Tucker . . . number thirty-four . . . batting for . . ."

He came up to the plate, the fans still yelling as he went into the box, loyally waving at him, thus making it harder to sight the ball in the fading light. He waited a second, stepped back, knocked the dirt from his spikes, and took his place once more. The pitcher wound up and whipped in the first one, straight at his chin. Roy whirled, stumbled, fell over onto the dirt, his bat rolling away.

Well, things are sure getting back to normal when they start knocking me down at the plate, he thought. Standing there, he dusted off his pants and took the wood from the bat boy. Now then, let's see what this guy's got.

The next ball fooled him completely. The pitcher powdered a fast one by him for a strike. He swung all the way round; he really went after it, but his timing was slow and he missed, as the crowd roared. Then came the one he wanted, a curve whipped in above the knees and over the corner. He met the ball, pulled it gently down the line, and was off toward first.

As he raced ahead he saw the first baseman had been caught cold. The pitcher had to come across, scoop it up, and throw all in one motion. Consequently his hurried toss was low and wide, getting away from the man on the bag. Roy without pausing in his stride took a sharp turn around first, his spikes gnawing holes in the basepath, and lit out for second. This was going to be close, awfully close, so he slid in with a hook through a storm of dust, once again drawing a quick throw that was low and difficult for the fielder to handle.

Watching as he slid in, Roy realized at once that the ball was getting away from the man above him and dribbling behind into open territory. Without checking his slide, he rose in one movement, came up and was off for third, while shortstop, second baseman, and fielder chased the ball. He was in pay dirt now, with Charlie, back of the bag, yelling at him to slide. Determined not to be caught, he roared into third and flung himself with a perfect tumble for the corner of the bag. Actually the throw was high enough so that the fielder never even reached for him.

He stood there panting, wiping off his monkey suit, the sweet music from the fans in his ears, the bleachers in deep center fermenting with excitement. Yes, the doctor was right. He was as fast as ever.

The harassed pitcher held a conference with his manager. Then he passed Swanson. It was good tactics, for one run would win and the old reliable was always a dangerous man. Next he went to work on Young.

With men on first and third, no one out, and the fans shrieking their heads off on every side, the pitcher stood there, impassive as though it was his first inning on the mound. Then he warmed up. A slider over the corner, a wasted ball round Lester's neck, a fast ball that was smoke, a curve that broke with Young's bat on his shoulder—and that was that. Lester went back to the bench.

Alan Whitehouse walked up to the plate. The pitcher stood in the box with his hands on his hips, glancing at Roy on third and Swanny on first, surveying the best pinch-hitter in the league, needed now if ever. Alan took the first two pitches, a strike and a ball. Then Charlie Draper put on the hit-and-run. Roy rubbed the left leg of his pants to show he had the sign, and danced up and down the baseline in foul territory, so as not to be struck by a batted ball.

He was off with that full-sounding smack of bat on ball, only to hear Charlie's warning shriek behind him. Realizing it was a fly, he dug in, turned, came back and tagged up. The ball was hit to left field, a good average fly, not deep, and not a short one either. Roy got set five feet back of the bag along the foul line, watching closely over one shoulder. Then he turned. Taking a running start, he hit the bag exactly the second the ball was caught, and struck out for home with every ounce he had.

That everything depended upon him he knew. This was their chance, this was their big moment, because Spike had no good pitcher left to put in if the game continued. That the throw-in would be close he was sure, because the Cub left fielder had one of the best arms in baseball. So he gave it the works. Forgotten was his weak leg and the months of pain and agony behind him. He only thought of the run they needed and the plate ahead.

On a play of this kind, most runners "put their heads down and go," as the old-timers say. Not Roy

Tucker. He had been taught always to keep his wits about him and watch for the whereabouts of the ball. Instead of running head down, full tilt for the plate, as he charged toward home he kept his eyes upon the catcher. Seeing the receiver's position, he instantly saw that a straight slide would be sure death. So ignoring a possible injury, he hurled himself forward, rolling toward the right side of the platter, reaching for it with outstretched arm. Above was the catcher, slashing round, lunging for him in vain.

CHAPTER

21

THE windows were high up along one wall of the big room, about halfway to the lofty ceiling. Around three sides were the lockers, six feet high and open in front, with a shelf near the top. There was a large weighing machine beside the door, and to the left as you entered was a small room with two rubbing tables and the Doc's electric diathermy machine. Back of it was Spike's dressing room, separated from the players' quarters by a wire grill. And to the left of the main door was a large blackboard, with a chalked notice written on it.

TRAIN LEAVES GRAND CENTRAL FOR ST. LOUIS TO-NIGHT AT 9:00 P. M. ALL UNIFORMS TO BE HANDED IN AFTER THE GAME. MGR.

The blue trunks with the red borders and the big letters in paint on the sides: BROOKLYN BASEBALL CLUB, were in the middle of the floor, half filled with clean uniforms. Near the outer door stood the bat trunk, ready to be hauled onto the field as soon as the game was over, for the bats to be stacked inside. Everything spoke of departure, of travel. The team was on the road again.

The Dodgers were off to battle abroad. But it wasn't the same ballclub that it had been three weeks previously. Things happen fast in Flatbush. That 9-game lead looked as safe as a church in mid-July. To catch the Dodgers, as Casey remarked, would take a writ of mandamus. It all seemed so easy then with everyone loose and confident, but when the first week of August rolled round and that margin had been peeled off to a couple of games, it wasn't quite so nice. Now the worst of the summer lay ahead, the intolerable heat of the middle west, with the whole National League hotter than a three-alarm fire. For only twelve games separated the first and eighth place clubs, and three of them, the Giants, the Cubs, and the Cards, all within a few games of the top, were breathing heavily down the Dodgers' tanned necks.

What had happened?

Yanking at his pants in his room after the game, Spike glumly tried to explain things to Casey and two reporters assigned to the club from the New York papers. The Dodgers had just blown their sixth straight game. You could feel the tension in the clubhouse as the men trooped in, disappointed and disgusted.

"Why, no, Jim, frankly, I don't agree. It isn't any disgrace to lose to those Cubs; they're a fine ballclub right now. Sure, we beat them in Chicago badly the last trip; they were in a slump. O.K., we're in a slump now. What of it? Haven't we got a right to one slump a season? The Giants had theirs in the spring, the Cards had theirs in June, and the Cubs in July. We'll work out of it, same as the others did.

"How's that, Roscoe? Sure we've been held up by injuries. Jocko Klein split his thumb on a foul tip. My brother's legs? Well, they're a bit rusty after four years in the service; why wouldn't they be? I realize with Swanny suffering from a charley horse that the right side of the infield looks like a sieve now. Frank Havens hasn't really panned out on first the way I hoped either. Don't print that, fellas; don't print that, please. We'll fight back—you wait and see."

Spike Russell never quit on his team, especially for publication. Yet that night in his compartment on the Southwestern he was gloomy. Surrounded by his brain-trusters, Charlie Draper and Red Cassidy, the coaches, and Fat Stuff, the wise old pitcher, he felt low. Things were worse than he really cared to admit in public.

"Le's see now, who does that leave for Cincinnati?"

"Mike's out until Monday with a cold; the Doc says Jerry Fielding is coming down with one too."

"I wish air conditioning had never been invented. You lose more pitchers through colds caught in air-conditioned rooms than through sore arms."

"We used Raz day before yesterday, and you were saving Ed Stone for the Reds. They hate knuckle-balls and he has a good one."

"Spike, why not let me take another crack in Cincinnati? I always had good luck there."

"You, Fat Stuff? Why, you were supposed to be a relief pitcher. Shucks, you've been starting more games this last month than the kids."

"That's O.K. with yours truly."

"I don't like the idea. Things really are tough when you get to using a relief pitcher regularly. Hang it all, Charlie, I thought shaking up the batting order might help. Then what happens? Young comes up with two on in the ninth and a chance to win the game, and . . ."

"Strikes out!" Charlie Draper lit a cigar. "Spike, let me tell ya, I never knew it to fail. When you have a guy in your line-up who isn't hitting, it makes no diff where you hide him. He's sure to come up when he can do you the most harm."

"Right!" said the old pitcher. "And lemme tell you, if he doesn't strike out he hits into a double-play. Well, I dunno about you fellas, but I'm all played out. Guess I'll turn in." He stood up. "Don't you worry, Spike. We got you out of worse holes than this; we'll yank you out of this one in a week. Watch our dust when we start to move."

Trouble, however, is hard for a losing club to shake. Paul Roth, who had been fielding brilliantly in left and had been up with the leading hitters in the league all season, came down with Lester Young's disease and fell into a batting slump. Frank Havens, the rookie on first, cost them a game in St. Louis by a bad error at a critical moment, and was far from a steadying influence over the infield. But good first sackers aren't a dime a dozen in mid-season, so Spike simply had to make the best of it. Then in Chicago the whole thing blew up.

They opened with a double-header against the Cubs, pacing the National League at the moment and only a game and a half back. The accumulated pressure of too much work caught up with Raz Nugent, and he found himself in trouble in the first game. Before Fat Stuff could warm up and get in to put out the fire, the Bruins were ahead, 8 to 5, and finally won the game by that score.

The second game was a heart-breaker. Earl Wingate, the Chicago star, was tieing the Brooks in knots, handcuffing the hitters, doing everything but making them throw their bats away. Young Jerry Fielding was almost as effective. It was, in fact, a replica of that extraordinary game in Brooklyn, with no score up to the eighth inning.

Then in the Cub's at bat, with two away and Jerry completely master of the situation, the batter hit a high foul near the right field stands. The ball seemed to be dropping into the boxes, so Havens ran over a few yards, stopped, and stood watching. Actually, the wind brought it back and it fell just inside the railing. The boxes in Wrigley Field are on a level with the field and it would have been easy to have reached over and snared that fly. On the next pitch, the batter pulled one down the right field line for two. Jerry became upset. He lost control momentarily, passed the next man, and then the catcher came up to clear the bags with a triple to the center field bleachers that Lester Young played badly. The final score was 2-0. The Cubs led the league by half a game.

It was after supper when Roy walked down the corridor to his room in the Edgewater Beach Hotel where the club was staying. An evening thunderstorm was coming in from the lake, and the wind happened to blow open a door at one side, disclosing an amazing spectacle. A big chap in shirt sleeves stood swinging a bat before a mirror. There was a puzzled frown on his forehead. He turned as the door banged, to see Roy standing there in the hallway.

"Roy! See here a minute, boy. Look at me, tell me what I'm doing wrong, will ya? You know, I heard of golfers fixing up their troubles by swinging before a mirror, so I brought this-here bat back with me tonight. Darned if I can figger out what's wrong." Lester Young stood there, stepping and swinging, stepping and swinging, stepping and swinging. Then he sank despondently into a chair.

"Twenty for one! Say, I bet that's about the worst record any Dodger had for years. Why, I haven't got a hit for so long I'll need a guide to show me the way to first base. I've tried everything but nothing works. Had a million tips telling me what to do; wandered about looking for hairpins and a load of barrels, only the women don't wear hairpins any more, and the boys, looks like they all drink beer out of bottles."

Roy laughed. "Les, you sure got yourself all tied up, haven't you? I was the same way when I first came up to the big club."

"You were! I always figgered you were a born hitter."

"No, sir, I wasn't a born hitter. I made myself, I taught myself to hit. Lester, I picked up your bat the other day. It's light. Why don't you use Swanny's club; you're strong enough to use that bat of his. Go up there and put the wood on the ball."

"Mebbe I could. That won't get me out of this slump."

"Well, I watched you last few games; I wonder

[171]

isn't your timing off. Think perhaps you're striding too soon. Hit what you see, don't anticipate too much; when it gets over the plate, swing. This'll keep you from striding too soon. Watch that ball; you know how 'tis, even the best hitters get a spell when they take their eyes off it. You're a good batter, must be some reason you fell off. I watched you at the plate; I think that's it."

Lester grabbed the bat from the corner again, stepped forward, and swung it before the mirror. "By ginger, I believe you got something there, Kid, I really do." He stepped once more, swinging the bat again and again. Then he turned.

"Ya know, Roy, we'd be well out in front in this race if I'd done any hitting at all the past month. I believe I'll snap out of it. Say, you're an okay guy to help me when I'm grabbing your spot on the club . . . and all . . ."

The door shut with a bang. "Nope, Lester, that's not the way to look at it. What helps you, helps us all. I'll get my cut of the Series dough if we win, whether I'm a regular or not. That's how the boys are; they'll vote it to me, that's the spirit on this-here club. Last year, Spike had no third baseman, so he yanks Swanny in from right field. That guy isn't young any more; likely you've noticed he always wears a hat; his hair is thin on top. He was a star when I came up before the war. Well, it would have got some men down to leave that nice quiet spot in right for the hot corner, to break into a new position at his age, and in the middle of the season, too. You know, a fella takes lots of pounding round third, and lemme tell you, Lester, that old whip of his saved us more than one game. Yes, sir, it's why we ended up in the first division."

A knock, short, sharp. They stood there, Roy by the bed, Lester before the mirror, bat in hand.

"Come in."

The door opened. Spike Russell stood there, a bunch of papers in his hand. He glanced at them both, at Lester's bat. They looked at him, at the furrow over his forehead which had deepened in the past few months. He nodded to each.

Roy immediately started toward the door. "Hello there, Spike. Good night, Lester."

The manager came in and shut the door. "Hold on a second. This concerns you both. Roy, you're going back in at your old spot tomorrow. Lester, I'm putting you on first."

Back again! Back with the boys. Down inside was

a warm feeling, a glow that enveloped Roy, a feeling so deep he could not think of one thing to say. Back with the crowd, back in there with the team, fighting. His hand was on the doorknob. Then his eyes caught Lester's face and his expression of bewilderment and disgust. Roy stood there a moment, looking. "O.K., Skipper, good night." He was gone.

Lester turned immediately. "Look here, Spike, you can't . . . I mean . . . I can't . . . I mean, I haven't played any at first for years now. I'm an outfielder . . . I came up as an outfielder . . . this batting slump won't last . . . I can't . . . shucks, I don't wanna . . ."

The young manager with the old look around his tired eyes came over and sat down on the bed. He tucked one leg under his knee, lit a cigarette, and reached for an ashtray. "Sit down, Lester. This is one club where you do what you're told!"

"Yeah? Zat so! Looka here, Spike Russell, get this, will ya? I don't hafta play for you or anyone else. I can go back to Milwaukee tomorrow. Just don't kid yourself . . ."

"Don't kid *yourself*, Lester, like you've been doing quite some time now. Lemme tell you a few things. We need a first baseman real bad, someone we can throw at with confidence. It's been our weak spot all season. First-off, at the start of the year, I tried Denny Pownall. He couldn't hit high school pitching, so we brought Havens up from Montreal. Today he played that fly ball as if it was loaded; that rockhead cost us the second game by not running for the foul there back of first. If we're not tryers on this club, we're nothing. There's no place here for a man who doesn't try. So he's out. I think you can be made into a better than average first sacker. I think when you get your eye in again and shake this slump, that with a big chap like you covering the bag and helping us out at the plate, with Roy rampaging in center once more, we can win that old pennant."

Some of Lester's anger had gone. "Yeah. I see, I know all that. But, Spike, I don't like to play first, never did; they's too much doing . . ."

"Too much responsibility, hey! I getcha. Lester, that boy Tucker who just left here; got an idea why he's back on the club again?"

"Sure. He's one great ballplayer."

"You are, too. But he's more than that; he's a bear-down guy from way back, that's what he is. From the things they tell me—I wasn't with the

[175]

Brooks then—Roy was a better than average hurler when he came up. But an injury ruined his arm. So what? He learned to bat and play the outfield, and the year before he went into the service he led the league. Then he had that-there crash in France and bust up his back. Why, he didn't even walk for several months last spring. But he refused to quit. Yeah, just as simple as that. He fought his way back. Now what? There he is on the varsity again.

"Here's something else, too. He's got something inside him, something way down deep, mebbe because he's always had to fight. He's been hurt, been laid off, and had to make good in spite of his injuries. And he did, too. That kinda does something to a man. Ever hear of that boy Weilander on the Braves? Had to have a finger of his throwing hand cut off at the knuckle; a drive fractured his finger when he was chucking batting practice one day. Well, he had a leather contraption made to protect the rest of his finger, and he's up there with the best of the pitchers on their club today. And this boy Scott of the Senators; lost a foot in a bomber over Berlin, gets an artificial one made, comes back, and darned if he isn't as fast as anyone on the club."

"Yeah, believe I heard of him."

"Lester . . . look, your trouble is it's all been too easy."

The big fellow was genuinely surprised. He hadn't expected anything of the sort. "Too easy? How you mean?"

"That's what I mean—too easy. These guys like Tuck come up the hard way, and it does something to 'em; it sorta puts the iron into 'em; it gives 'em something you haven't got. Look at Jocko Klein. Same thing. The boys like to hound the living daylights out of him his first year up 'cause he was Jewish. One day he waded into them and fought back. They let up and quick too, and what is he today? Just about the best catcher in baseball, that's all. He's got guts."

"Oh, sure, he has. Never said he hadn't."

"Now you"—Spike paid no attention—"it's all been too easy for you. First, you're a natural hitter, you can't miss. You got everything. Couple of years on Little Rock, then Milwaukee where you lead the league, and bang! Jack puts down twenty-five grand for you, sight unseen. Greatest rookie of the year. You crowd Roy Tucker clean off the club. You burn up the circuit. You're in all the write-ups and interviews in every city we come to. What's it Casey called you? The Million Dollar Baby. And girls, dozens of 'em. Oh, sure, I watched 'em line up there at Ebbets Field for your autograph. I know you have a girl or two in every city on the circuit. Wonder I found you in tonight."

"No, Spike, you got me wrong, honest to goodness, you got me wrong."

"I know what time the boys get to bed, Lester. You've been half ruined, what between the girls and the sportswriters. Now, at last, you find yourself up against a tough proposition. It isn't so easy. You fall into a slump, you get jittery, and when I ask you to play first you blow up and talk of going back to Milwaukee. Yah! Look, Lester . . ."

He leaned over and put out his cigarette. His face was close to the big chap in the easy chair who shuffled the bat nervously between his knees.

"Look, Lester, remember the run Roy Tucker scored for us when we beat Wingate in that extra-inning game at home, remember? He risked everything for that one run. He had no idea would his leg stand up when he struck out for home plate that time. He didn't know would he ruin himself for good, and he didn't care, either. We had to have that run. O.K., he went out and got it for us. That's the way we play on this ballclub." He rose and went toward the door.

"Unless you do the same thing, unless you quit chasing round with the girls, there's no spot open here. You can get your ticket to Milwaukee from the secretary tomorrow morning. Go out there at first or go home. Make up your mind. Good night, Lester."

"Er . . . er . . . good night, Spike."

CHAPTER

22

═══════

CASEY sauntered into the dugout late the next day. It was just before game time, but he had been delayed in reaching the park. He sat kidding with the boys, his favorite pastime; for he had discovered that jokes and laughter were often more productive of copy than serious discussions about pitchers' arms and the technical side of baseball. That afternoon he was giving it back and forth with Raz Nugent, the sportswriter and the ballplayer furnishing entertainment to the entire bench.

"No use talking, Raz, you ain't what you used to be!"

"Nope. Well, who is?" rejoined the big pitcher philosophically.

"Yes, sir, if it wasn't for that salary whip of yours,

Razzle, you'd be back in overalls on your farm down in South Carolina."

"Yeah, maybe." The ballplayer was never at a loss for a retort. "And if it wasn't for that-there type-writer of yours, you wouldn't be a baseball writer, you'd be driving a truck at thirty bucks a week."

The whole bench laughed. Casey didn't particularly enjoy the laughter. "I'm not a baseball writer, you ham," he reminded Razzle. "I'm a sports columnist. I do a daily column; write football and other sports. If you could read, Raz, you'd understand the difference."

The big hurler picked up his glove, winked at Roy sitting opposite him on the dugout step, and rose with dignity. He climbed from under the roof, stepped out on the field, a look of acute distaste upon his face. Taking a ball, he spit copiously into his glove and walked away, yanking down his cap. Then he half turned to the bench again, and called back over one shoulder: "A football writer, hey! A football writer is a baseball writer with a vest on."

Laughter rocked the bench. "Isn't that guy something!"

"Can't get ahead of old Raz."

"They don't make 'em like him any more!"

"They sure don't, these kids coming along haven't any personality."

"I remember when he first joined the club. He blew into our hotel in Florida before the war; 'twas a Sunday, and in those days you couldn't play baseball down there on Sundays. Raz now, he rolled into the lobby"—Fat Stuff pulled off his cap and ruffled his thick black hair with his fingers—"wearing a sweater and an old, dirty pair of pants. So naturally someone asked him was he going to play golf that afternoon.

"Raz, he sets down his battered tin suitcase with the bat strapped to one side, and says, solemn-like: 'Golf! Mister, you got me wrong; I'm Raz Nugent, the ballplayer.'"

"Yep, and that's what he's been ever since," chimed in Charlie Draper. "Dave Leonard was managing the club that season, and when he sees Raz in the lobby, he takes him to his room and says, sort of explaining, 'Nugent, mebbe you better put on a shirt to come to the dining room tonight.' Raz, he just looked at Dave. 'Shirt! You mean one of them things they wear a tie with? I didn't never have one of them things on.'"

"Yeah, and now look at him. Every time he steps

outside of his room he looks like Mr. Esquire with a new suit on and three hundred bucks of clothes over his shoulders."

CLANG-CLANG-CLANG. The bell stung the bench into activity, the boys getting ready for battle, while Casey rose to make the long climb up to the press box, pausing en route for a quick luncheon of coffee and a couple of hot dogs. He did not actually reach his colleagues above until the first half of the inning was over, and the Brooks were about to take the field. Wedging into an empty space in the long line of sportswriters, he uncorked his typewriter, struck a match to light a cigarette, and then hesitated as the Dodgers ran onto the diamond.

He sat there staring down, the unlit cigarette drooping from his lips. The match burned down in one upraised hand. "For Pete's sake! There's Roy Tucker back in center again. They've benched Lester . . . no . . . suffering polecats! Lester Young on first! Is that Young on first there? Hey, Mike, hey, Sam, why didn'ya tell me?"

A chorus of angry cries rose along the press box, and the clattering of a dozen typewriters slowed down for a few seconds. Their replies had a trace of annoyance in them.

[183]

"He never told *us*. We never knew no more'n you did until they went out to practice before the game." As one man, the entire press box then turned back to their machines and the clattering telegraph keys at their side. This was news. The Dodgers' line-up was being revamped with the end of the season only a month distant.

Next morning Casey's column dealt at length with the team, now precariously sitting with a half a game lead in the National League.

"It wasn't so much that they won the last game of the series with the Cubs at Wrigley Field yesterday, or the way they won it, as the fact that Spike Russell finally seems to have his team in hand for the down-to-the-wire sprint in the pennant race. The fundamentals of a ballclub are through the middle: catcher, pitcher, shortstop and center fielder. He has them all. Yesterday Roy Tucker went back to his old spot in the middle garden, which is bad news for enemy hitters. Yesterday in Chicago Roy played as if his leg had never bothered him at all.

"Handling two difficult singles with dispatch and holding the runners each time to one base, the Kid from Tomkinsville snared two fly balls in his region, and made a really fine professional catch off one.

This was hit by Cy Ashwell, a ball that forced Swanson and Roth over; but Tuck raced in and gloved it smoothly. In the 8th he got hold of a high inside pitch at the platter, and laced it to right for a smart single that scored the winning run. Roy always likes to bat in a crucial spot of this kind; he bears down a little extra. He's a ballplayer's ballplayer, and will be a tonic for the Bums in the tough days ahead.

"Spike Russell made other changes and apparently to the good. He gave Frank Havens his unconditional release, for the former Montreal Royal hasn't been shaping up any too well in the big time, and the coaches consider he isn't yet ready for the majors. Spike placed Lester Young on first. The big chap played the base mostly by ear yesterday; but he was in there trying every minute, and saved the ballgame in the ninth when he jumped into the air to snare Shiell's throw, a catch only possible because of his height and his quick, long reach. It was the play of the afternoon.

"At the dish, he powdered the ball cleanly and met it squarely each time he came to bat. Unfortunately his rifled shots were going straight at the opposing fielders until the ninth, when he backed

Milton Arnstein up against the barrier in deep left with a stinger that missed being a home run by a very few feet. When these blows start falling into open territory, as they will some day, the rest of the league better watch out. Meanwhile, after a few more practice sessions, Lester may become a useful first sacker and plug up the hole in the infield which has been worrying Spike and his coaches all season.

"Last night the Bums left for Pittsburgh by air, where they tackle the Pirates in a four-game series at Forbes Field beginning this afternoon. They are still squeezing that slender lead of half a game, with the Cards, Cubs and Giants all within three games or less of the leaders. Sunday's double-headers can mean lots of changes in the standing. The race is a double-jointed doosey."

23

GUESSING is all part of the business, yet rarely, if ever, had Casey been so exact in his prophecies. That Sunday's double-header caused many shake-ups in the club standing. The Cards and the Cubs, playing second-division teams, each won a couple. The Giants took two also, the nightcap in 14 innings, while the Dodgers dropped two to the Pirates, and found themselves traveling home in fourth place, the lowest berth they had occupied since early May. Late that afternoon the Cards were perched precariously atop the league, a game ahead of the Cubs. Only a few percentage points separated the four first-division teams.

Spike Russell was worried now. There had been plenty of times during the season when the team looked bad, when they'd slump so it seemed they never would shake it off, and then bang! They'd slash into some league-leading pitcher or smash into one of those do-or-die affairs to maintain their slender lead. Tossing in his compartment on the train that night, he lay awake as Altoona and Tyrone and Harrisburg flashed past in the dark, realizing that this was a turning point for the club, replaying the season, game by game, thinking of the close ones they'd lost by a single run, by that one bobble in the field, by that ball striking on the wrong side of the foul line.

We can't go on like this, we really can't. We never failed to win the game we needed to stay on top until this afternoon. Well, the boys'll either come back as they've invariably done, or else slump into the second division, and fast. Tucker, he's my man out there; he's a manager's ballplayer. And Lester begins to look at home on first. But the pitchers! Well, it's anyone's race now. The thing is wide open.

Ordinarily Monday was an open date for all clubs, but the Dodgers had to play a postponed game at the Polo Grounds the next afternoon, to be followed by a series of four at Ebbets Field against New York. The brain trust talked things over as they dressed in the manager's room of the clubhouse the next day, concentrating on the game ahead. They all knew if this one was lost, their chances of getting back into first place again were none too good. Charlie Draper made the remark they all had in their minds:

"What we need is a stopper—some pitcher, someone who can go in there and stop any opponent, some big guy who can be counted on to take the crucial game in a series. That's if we're gonna stay up there with 'em. Raz Nugent is tired; he's worn down. Jerry's too young to be depended on in the clutch. Mike has that bum shoulder. Eddie? Sure, but you can't pitch him every day in the week like you've been doing lately. He's tired, too."

"With Jerry being in and out, and Doc giving Mike injections for his torn back muscle every time he pitches . . . and Raz no use, as you say, I don't see your stopper on this staff."

"I see him!" Old Fat Stuff spoke and they listened. "Why not shoot a wire to Montreal, Spike?"

"Montreal?"

"You mean Bonesey?"

"He's undependable. Always behind the hitters."

"He won 14 and 4 up there, and they're on top.

Can't do that and be behind the hitters. Maybe he's learned his lesson."

"Aw, MacManus doesn't like Bonesey; never did."

"Yeah? Jack wants to win the pennant, doesn't he?"

"Besides, you're the manager. We need him bad; what say, Charlie?"

"Why, I think you got something, Fat Stuff. If that kid behaves, he can win from five to seven games for us between now and the end. That would just about mean the old flag."

"Right," said Spike. "I'll wire for him this afternoon and tell Jack I did it. Bones might even catch the night plane and go in against this southpaw of theirs tomorrow. All right, Charlie, get the gang together."

It was a quiet meeting and short that afternoon. The boys were sober, worried and anxious like their chief, as they sat round facing him in the cool clubhouse. Roy noticed the circles under the eyes of the manager, the taut expression about his mouth, knew he had slept little the previous night. And no wonder. When your team falls off the ladder after being up there all season, it's not easy to keep cool and unruffled.

"Fellas, there's nothing to go over in those two games against Pittsburgh yesterday. That big lefty sure pitched ball the first game, and as for the second, well, what is there to say about a 9-0 beating? They just clubbed us to death, that's all. Every team runs into that sort of thing at times and bounces right back the next day. Forget it. We've always snapped back and we will this time. We're not first any more; what of it? The strain is on the team that has to watch the scoreboard; that'll be the Cards now. Let them try it for a change.

"But no use kidding ourselves, either this is our series or we're through. We must win to stay in there. Playing the Giants on their home grounds is always tough; but we've had the edge on 'em here all season. Don't forget, fellas, that Jameson and Tonelli hit to either field. Last time we pitched to Jameson, he hit to left, center, and right on three consecutive trips to the plate. Lester, play that ball, move so you'll get a good hop, charge it, don't ever let it play you the way you did once yesterday.

"Now this man Jackson, he has a good change of pace and likes to use it. Don't let him fool you. Guess that's about all. Here's the line-up for today: Swanny, right. Russell, short. Lester, first. Tuck, center. Roth in left. Shiells, third. Bob on second, and Jocko catching. And Fat Stuff on the mound. All right then, guys, le's go get 'em."

There was a scraping of chairs and benches. Then they left the cool room smelling of arnica and the Doc's liniments, and tramped into the sunlight outside, down the long steps to the field. The stands, nearly full already, greeted them with a roar, for it was going to be almost a full house even on Monday.

And in each player's mind was the same thought: Fat Stuff! Gee, Spike is really scraping the barrel. But why's he throw in the old-timer right here? Why not hand 'em Jerry or Mike or even Raz? Fat Stuff! Well, he must know what he's doing, but it seems like an awful chance.

When the old-timer went out to warm up, the Giant bench was both amused and delighted. "The Brooks must be down to bedrock to hand us the old man at a time such as this." "Hey, look, Mac, he can just about get the ball to his warm-up catcher and no more." "We should grab off about three hits apiece from that daffy-dill he's pushing over." "Why, it's pitiful. He's just an old, crippled duck."

The first Giant hitter in the opening inning reached one of Fat Stuff's slow balls and singled smartly to left. Some wag upon the New York bench immediately remarked, "Well, there goes his no-hitter." They all roared with laughter. This was to be a pushover, the clincher for their hold on third place.

However, Spike knew what he was doing. Instead of entrusting that critical game and the task of subduing the onrushing Giants before their home crowd to a brilliant youngster who might blow up under pressure, he had called again on his veteran relief pitcher. The old man had little speed and not much of a curve, yet he had perfect control; he could put the ball where he wanted. He kept floating little dinkey-dinks up to the plate, balls that were almost a shot-put. But they invariably came in a tough spot for the batter. Low and inside; up around the shoulder—pitches that were all difficult to hit solidly. Time after time the Giants would get men on base, and the next man would pop up or go down swinging, throwing his bat toward the dugout in disgust. Inning succeeded inning, and the old hurler held them in check.

The Dodger hitters were not doing much better, and they were lucky to put over two earned runs in the fifth. At the last half of the ninth, they led

2-0. A round of applause swept the stands as Fat Stuff strolled out to the mound, for the fans all recognized his masterly pitching in the clutches. Far out in the bullpen, two Dodger hurlers resumed work. They had spent the afternoon rising and sitting down.

Tonelli, the first hitter, struck the initial pitch between short and third, but Spike saved things by dashing into the hole and throwing out the speedy Giant by a whisker. One down. Lester Young then hurled himself into the air and speared a terrific liner that was tagged. The fans started to leave the ball park, the tension that had hovered over the field all afternoon died off, the noise from the bleachers subsided. Out in the bullpen the throwing of the three Brooklyn relief pitchers became casual and desultory. They half turned, watching for the final out.

As always in baseball, trouble was there when least anticipated. The final out refused to come. One man worked a pass, the old pitcher finally losing him after a dozen balls were fouled off. The next batter beat out an infield grasscutter, and on the hit-and-run the following man rifled a pistol shot back through the mound. Racing in, Roy scooped up the ball and shot it home on the fly to Jocko. The Giant runner took no chances with one of the best throwing arms in baseball, and scuttled back to third after rounding the bag at full speed.

Now those relief pitchers out there were busy, throwing in earnest, quickly getting the ball back from the catchers, burning it in, fast, faster, faster. The fans who had been leaving settled into their seats again; others stood in the rear of the grandstand; they yelled, shrieked, shouted. A round of rhythmic clapping swept over the ball park. Clap-clap, clap-clap they went in unison, trying hard to rattle the old man in the box. Through it all he was ice-water. Then Spike and Jocko with his tools on and Charlie Draper gathered about him.

A clean single would tie the game. A slashing double would win it, for the winning run was on first. The little knot around the mound finally dissolved. Spike ran back to his position in deep short to play for a runner at any base. He was sticking with Fat Stuff.

A sort of murmur ran over the stands. "You sure gotta hand it to him." "He's a cool customer to stick with the old geezer in a spot like this."

The September shadows deepened over the park,

bisecting the diamond. The whole place was up yelling. On the mound the veteran picked up the rosin bag, dusted off his hands, tossed it away, looked about the bases loaded with runners, hitched at his pants and took the sign. He nodded, wound up, threw.

The batter took the pitch. Low; a ball. The crowd roared. He fouled off the next one, going for a downer. The third one he put the wood to—the clout of the afternoon.

"Yowser!" shrieked a player on the Giant bench. "It's a homer. I can tell by the sound of it."

The ball was hit cleanly and with strong wrists. It took off, and Roy in deep center knew by the sound of the bat there was power behind the blow. He took off too, the second it was struck, racing back full gallop, watching it over one shoulder. This meant the ballgame; perhaps the pennant if it fell safely, for the runners were rounding the bags. He dug in with everything he had. Far, far out toward the clubhouse in the rear he saw it falling, leaped in the air, and stuck out a desperate glove to one-hand it as it came down.

The Dodgers were in third place.

CHAPTER
24

EVERYONE on the club felt the strain. Nerves were tight; tempers short; the big men and the husky ones and the thin, wiry athletes were all played out under the strain. They stretched but they did not crack.

Yet the effort to come through each afternoon became harder and harder. In the morning when they rose, the day ahead seemed a mountain that had to be climbed with shoes weighing a hundred pounds apiece. Even Roy, who had played less than half the season, felt it. He lay on the rubbing table before the last game of the Giant series, his face buried in his arms, while the Doc, a small heat lamp in one hand, loosened up his aching leg.

"I feel like I usta in spring training in Florida,

Doc. Can't seem to get that spring-training ache out of my muscles."

The Doc waved the lamp professionally over Roy's hip and thigh, rubbing in liniment with the other hand. "That isn't surprising, Roy." Putting the lamp upon a small table at his left, he went to work on the leg with his two powerful hands. "Nope, that isn't surprising. You need a rest—same as every-one else on this club."

"A rest! Are you kidding? Why, I've hardly played half the season. Don't give me that; don't make me laugh, Doc."

"Just the same, it's what you need. Point is, you're using muscles now you haven't been using for a long time. That's the big difference; it's the trouble with Bobby Russell and every returning serviceman in the business."

Rest right at that moment was out of the question for anyone. They were in that last final charge to the wire when every ounce and every out counts, when the club that gets nine men pulling together each afternoon for nine innings would take the pennant and enter the Series. Having won three straight from the Giants, with Jerry pouring it on in the opener at Ebbets Field, and Raz winning the next

[198]

one, they needed only one more victory to be in second place. That was up to all of them—and especially to Bones Hathaway.

MacManus had objected to calling him back and then to using him, and it was only after much argument that Spike finally got the big chap cleared and ready for the final contest of the series. A huge crowd came out to welcome the star hurler back with the club. It was pitcher's weather that day—not too cold, and a wind from the northwest. That meant low visibility, the breeze blowing with the hurlers and against the home-run hitters. Even the Giants watched the newcomer warm up with interest. Truth to tell, Bonesey, surrounded by sportswriters and cameramen, didn't look so hot. Just another moundsman the desperate Dodgers were throwing in to stop that slide to the second division at any cost.

Several Giants came across and spoke to him, half-kidding, half-serious. "Glad to see you, Bonesey." "How's Montreal, Bones? Like it up there?" Once upon a time he had been their meat, once he had been their cousin, and the bench jockeys could be counted upon to make his temperature rise by sly references to his escapades of former years. So they weren't exactly sorry to see him again.

Old Fat Stuff, however, watching with shrewd glances from the top step of the dugout, his back against one of the pillars of the roof, missed little. "One thing that kid got at Montreal is a slider," he remarked quietly to Charlie, who stood in the dugout below.

To the unobservant, it wasn't the same Bonesey who had left them early in the season; he was calmer and more deliberate. But the moment he took the mound, the fans recognized the little tricks on the mound you could never forget—the digging in of the left foot; that sweeping warm-up, with the kick as the ball slid from his hand; the twist to his left knee as he fogged them past the Giants' bats at the plate.

Bones had always been speedy. That day his fast ball was smoke; his curve was so sharp you could shave with it. And he had learned things during his exile in the minors; he hadn't spent his time being sorry for himself in Montreal. His control was perfect. He struck out at least one man an inning and walked few. He had class. You couldn't explain it if you tried, but it stuck out all over him as inning followed inning and he kept setting the Giants back on their heels. In vain the New York bench jockeys jeered and sneered through cupped hands when he walked out to the box. In vain their sluggers strode up, fire in their eyes, teeth clenched, and a determined expression on every face. Bonesey was having none of it.

In the old press box, long since abandoned for that aerie perch on the roof, sat Jack MacManus, with a friend from Detroit who happened to be in town. A scowl was on his forehead as Bones took the box and the crowd roared, but it didn't stay there long as goose eggs mounted up on the scoreboard in right. Gradually his expression changed to a smile, then to a complacent look, then to a grin.

"He's always had a fast ball and a pretty fair curve. Now he has control, he's ahead of the hitters all the time. And he's throwing in a swell change of pace . . . see . . . see that! Just a great pitcher, that's all! I always said so. Mighty glad I insisted Spike bring him back. Well, I told this kid last spring when I sent him away, I said: 'Sonny, it's up to you. Entirely up to you. I have faith in you or I'd give you your release this morning; but whether we pick up your option again or not depends on you.' Those were my words, Tom, my very words." He indicated to his friend that he himself had really sent the wire recalling Bonesey from exile.

All through the game, however, the Dodgers themselves were hit-hungry. It was as though at the fag end of the season they were too tired even to stand up and slug the ball. They couldn't seem to buy a base hit; little pop-ups, rollers to the infield, and an occasional fly ball with one or two scattered bingles were their only contributions to victory at the plate. They were unable to put more than one man at a time on the bags, let alone threaten their adversaries. The Giant pitcher, a southpaw with a sweeping curve, had them helpless all through.

Then in the New York seventh, a sudden hilarious and joyful cry rose over the field. The figure 6 went up beside the Pirate score; the Cubs were being manhandled in Pittsburgh. This, then, was the clincher for second place. They had to take it now— or else. By this time the wind had died away, the flag in center field hung down from the pole, as Swanny, lead-off man for the Brooks, stepped to the plate. He dropped a blooper in right and reached first unmolested. The crowded stands began to stamp and cheer. It was the long-looked-for break at last.

Behind third, Charlie Draper clapped his hands. Swanny, on the bag, watched to see whether the take was on or off, and Lester, approaching the plate, glared from under the rim of his cap to get the signal. Charlie's leathery tones swept across the diamond, penetrating the crowd roar. He tugged at the visor of his hat, he kicked the dirt angrily with his spikes, he yelled across through cupped hands. The hit-and-run was on. And Swanny was away at the first move of the pitcher's arm.

Unfortunately, the Giants guessed that Swanny would go on the first ball. Accordingly, the pitch was high outside, almost too far away to hit. Lester waved vainly in an attempt to upset the catcher, who took the throw in his stride and pegged it on a line to second. Swanny, straining in desperation, slid into the bag, but the baseman had the tag on him and he was out. He rose, disconsolately dusting the dirt from his pants, shaking his head as he walked past Charlie to the bench. One down, and another rally nipped before it had begun.

Lester Young was sore, plenty sore at himself. For too long he had been a sucker at the plate. Red of face, cursing, he stepped aside, wiping his hands carefully on his shirt front, scooping up some dirt and rubbing it on the handle of his war-club. Then, waving his wand, he came back into the box. The big pitcher tried to blow a fast ball by him. It was a mistake. Lester was ready and waiting for just such a pitch.

He caught it squarely, sending it on a line into the hole between center and left. Expert fielding and a snappy relay held him up; but when they returned the ball to the infield he was standing on the pay-off post.

Something had happened. It was contagious. The electric atmosphere over the park, the stimulus of their comeback, perhaps those six runs on the scoreboard, and second place beckoning once again with open arms, that and the big crowd pulling for the run that might win the game, all of these together set the club afire at last. The bench became a hotspot. No one could sit still. They stood on the plank, leaning against the roof, roaring at Lester, at Roy stepping into the batter's box. A burst of pent-up energy, of their last nervous resources, was released like a fever through the whole line-up. One man after another felt it, one man after another showed it as he strode up to the platter.

[204]

"Whang!" went Roy Tucker's bat on the first pitch.

"Bang!" went Paul Roth's war-club on the second pitch.

"Wham!" went Frank Shiell's big stick on the third.

Charlie Draper in the coaching box became a madman. "Go on, Les, you ice cart, go on . . . go on, Tuck old boy; go on, Roy, see you on the bench . . . go on, Paul, you elephant, go on . . ."

"Slam!" went Bobby Russell's bat, which put the stopper to it all by clouting the ball over the right field fence into Bedford Avenue, and the Bums into second place. So close to the leading Cards it wasn't funny.

CHAPTER

25

A GAME and a half in the lead!

A game and a half is not much. Nothing at all, in
fact, in the spring when everyone is fresh and keen
and baseball is fun, when the clubs are all crowding
on each other's heels and everyone has a shot at the
old flag, and the long season stretches out in a dim
vista ahead. September is then a future so distant
you don't even think about it. A game or so isn't
much in midsummer either, although the fun has
long vanished and baseball by this time is a grind.
Because a game won or lost then can easily be
picked up later. A game isn't much even in late
August, when the injuries mount fast and the best
men are overworked and tired, and all the pitching
staff is thin and drawn; even then a game or so is
no great handicap.

But in the final weeks of the year a game and a half is as big as twenty.

One game and a half was the lead of the Dodgers in mid-September. They were facing their favorite whipping boys, the tired Phils, with whom they had won seventeen and lost four that season. Whereas the desperate Cards were forced to slug it out against the tough third-place Cubs in a double-header in Chicago, with that game and a half deficit staring them in the face all afternoon.

The pennant surge of the Brooks those golden September days had swept them to the front, kept them there, too. The result was fever in Flatbush. All Brooklyn—and all Manhattan too—apparently wanted to be on hand that afternoon. The gang formed unusually early at the window. There were many empty offices, many vacant seats in more than one school that morning, with their owners in line at Ebbets Field, arguing about their favorites, waiting for the gates to open.

"Tell ya, Swanny can't carry Tucker's glove."

"Can't, hey! Yeah, and who ast him to? He has to play the line, Swanny does."

"Play the lines! Play the lines! The lines are a cinch. The lines aren't tough to play. The center fielder, now, he's right in the middle of everything, he has to cover up both holes, he has to watch for hits through the middle."

"Hey! There goes Spike Russell and his brother, too. Hey there, Spike! Hi, Bobby, hi!"

Spike Russell, young in years yet old in baseball experience, knew that they could lose that important game, knew anything might happen. And warned his men in the clubhouse before they took the field.

"Sure, sure we're sitting pretty. Sure the pressure is on the Cards; only let's us not take anything for granted. Let's go right after 'em hard from the start. Pay no attention to those Redbirds. Don't watch the scoreboard. Never mind what happens out there in the west. Play this game here, today. Maguire most likely will chuck Spencer at us; he's beaten some good clubs this season. He's won twelve for a tail-end team and he's two and two against us. He's a crooked arm pitcher, throws curves and nothing but, has a good change of pace; he's dangerous, so watch out. We beat him before, and the way we've been going lately no reason why we can't do it again. O.K. For Pete's sake, hit 'em and hit 'em hard at the start; give everything you got the first few innings. Let's build up a lead for Ed right away. And le's go get 'em!"

Baseball is a funny game. When you least expect a battle, there it is. Eddie Stone that afternoon was tough and confident, fast in his warm-up, with a hook that was sliding off the inside in a threatening manner. The team trotted out behind him, smooth and easy, a pennant-winning ballclub ready for anything.

When the first Philly batter went down swinging, the vast crowd settled back with delight. Wasn't this the thing they had come for? Then followed one of those breaks. The next hitter smacked a grass-cutter toward Bob Russell. He came racing in, scooped it up cleanly, and there was a race for the bag between ball and runner. The throw nailed him by a whisker. But the hands of the umpire were down.

"Aw . . . *no!*"

"He was out a country mile!"

"Hey there, Stubblebeard . . ."

The decision was so close that ordinarily it would-n't have bothered any of them. But this was no ordinary contest. This was a time when every out counted twice over. When nerves were close to the surface, when everybody on the club was edgy, when a matter of four or five thousand dollars rode on every pitch.

They surrounded the umpire, protesting the decision, yelling and shouting. The old man folded his arms majestically and stalked away. While the batter stood serenely perched on first.

Eddie was annoyed. He threw down his glove in disgust, tight and tense under the strain. He kicked angrily at the rosin bag as he came back into the box, and shook off Jocko who strolled out to calm him down. As a result he lost the next man. Two on, and the stands apprehensive. This wasn't what they had been standing in line since early morning to see.

The third batter hit the ball solidly. Roy, standing like a sprinter with his right foot forward, timed it perfectly and was off at the crack of the bat. Going back, two steps, five steps, ten steps, he turned at precisely the right moment, and gloved it for the out. The stands became jubilant again. Two down. This was more like it.

Two out and the situation easier, although the Phils' only good batter was striding to the plate. The picket line moved slightly around to left as

Eddie went to work carefully. Two balls were fouled off, two were taken. On the next pitch, the batter reached for a high curve and lifted a lazy fly to left, well within the lines and over toward the stands. Frank Shiells, the third baseman, was off instantly, so was Spike, and so was Paul Roth. But it was the third baseman's ball if anyone's.

The blow was a twisting, teasing fly that angled off toward the boxes. Shiells dug in hard, while Roth on one side and Spike nearing him on the other yelled warnings.

"Watch out, Frank!"

"Look out, look out!"

He heard their voices distinctly above the crowd roar, but he was going to get that ball. It was falling now, falling fast. He reached for it, lunged, missed, tripped and fell over against the iron rail of the field box, tumbling to the ground. His head struck the rail as he went down, and he lay there while his teammates gathered round.

The crowd rose, stretching to peer down, anxious to discover the extent of the disaster. The stretcher came out, and he was laid on it carefully and taken away. The stands rose as he went past; there were

[211]

some scattered handclaps which died away. Alan Whitehouse ran to Shiells' spot at third.

"Whitehouse, No. 6, for Shiells, No. 18, at third."

Now Eddie was really upset. On the 2 and 2 pitch he tried to sneak in a fast one. It was the wrong moment. The batter out-guessed him, and promptly lined it over the fence into Bedford Avenue. Three runs to the bad, and their star third sacker out of the game. While over in Chicago, as the scoreboard showed, the rampaging Redbirds were slaughtering the Cubs in the first game of their double-header, drawing closer and closer to the leaders in that hectic finish. Three runs; three runs to the bad and Shiells out, perhaps for good. The crowd was rocked.

"We don't lose to the Phillies; why, it isn't possible!"

"We don't lose to those icemen."

Spencer, for Philadelphia, was at his best when he had to be. Working coolly and efficiently behind that 3-0 lead, he throttled the anxious Brooks at every turn, forcing Bob Russell to hit into a double-play with two on and one out in the third. In the fifth, after Lester Young had spanked a triple and Paul Roth sent him home with a long fly to deep center, Roy and Spike both singled, but the Philadelphia pitcher put the brakes on the rally by making Al Whitehouse and Bob pop up weakly to the infield.

Spike masterminded all over the place. In the last of the fifth he removed Eddie for a pinch-hitter; in the seventh he took out Mike Mehaffey and replaced him for another pinch-hitter. He ordered his men about the diamond, tried hit-and-runs to squeeze in a couple of scores. In the ninth the Brooks staged one of those typical last-minute surges and came within an inch of winning. With one down and men on first and third, and the stands in a frenzy all over the park, Swanny brought a roar of delight as he belted a liner at the box which was really hit. The roar began . . . and died away.

The ball struck the pitcher on the ankle, caromed off into the hands of the shortstop, and a rapid double-play snuffed out the last chance of the fighting Dodgers. Back in the clubhouse there was gloom.

"Hey there, give me another cold compress." "And out in Chicago, folks, those unstoppable Cards, after taking the first game, are cutting down the Cubs' lead in the second. And, folks, what a ballclub those Cards are! They just won't stay down. At the end of four innings, it is Chicago 4, St. Louis 3." "Hey there, Doc! How's Frank? He is?" "And now, folks, they musta got word about the game in Brooklyn, because those Cards really broke loose in the sixth." "Is he hurt much, Doc?" "Losing to those hillbillies! Cripes, what luck!" "That-there Stubblebeard calls hisself an ump." "How the Cards stand in the night-cap?" "Shiells out for good? He is?" "And, folks, in the eighth the Cards put the clincher on it. Homer Slawson plunked one over the fence with three men aboard, followed by Conlin, who . . . and that about ties up the pennant race." "Hey there, doctor, can you tell me how bad he's hurt?"

CHAPTER

26

"Who, me? Me take over the hot corner?"

"The hot corner! The hot corner! What's hot about it?" There was a trace of annoyance and more than a touch of fatigue in Spike's tones. "Old Grouchy used to say a third baseman stood in the shade and handled one chance all afternoon."

"Yeah, I know, I understand. It isn't that, Skipper. It's . . . well, I just couldn't, that's all."

Some players you can be tough with. Some players like Lester Young can be handled rough; you merely tell them where they get off. Roy Tucker was different. "Why not, Roy?" What on earth is biting the guy, anyhow? It was the first time Spike had ever asked something of the Kid from Tomkinsville and been turned down.

"Well, Spike, most probably you wouldn't understand. It's hard to explain." Why should he understand? It's like trying to tell folks about war; they listen and say yes at the right moment, but they haven't been through it themselves and they just can't realize what it's all about. "I couldn't manage at third base right now. I'd be saying how-do-you-do to the fast ones."

"What makes you think so, Roy?"

"I know it, Spike. See here now, I'm as quick on my feet as ever this season, when I get started. I can run all right, once I get under way. But you must have noticed I'm slow starting. I'm . . . well, I haven't got my confidence back yet; I can't get going fast; I can't jump in either direction the way I usta. I'm all right, but I'm not hauling in those three baggers like the old days. That'll come in time, that'll come as my back gets stronger and I get my confidence again, only it won't come right away. And my back isn't O.K. yet. I don't feel I can take chances on it. I'm not able to do things I'll find easy next year when it's stronger. One twist or a sudden strain, and bang! There she goes! Twists and starts, that's about all third base is, Skipper."

Spike said nothing. He sat there looking at him

closely, seeing a different Roy Tucker. Why, he's plain frightened. He's scared to go in there at third. He's afraid.

Yet somehow you don't say those things. You can't call a fellow a quitter who's been through what Roy has. Spike was puzzled.

"Roy, see here, if you don't take over at third it means bringing someone down from Montreal. You know what'll happen with a rookie on third base and the Cards coming into town day after to-morrow. Boy, we'll win the pennant—or lose it—in this series. In the first game, too, most likely. Give us that first game and they'll never catch us; they can't. If you take over, and Al Whitehouse goes to center, we're really set. He's a guy who may unload one into the bleachers any time. With Al in your spot, we'll go places. Otherwise . . ."

There was a long silence. He's plain scared; he doesn't dare to take a chance. He even admits it himself. This is sure a new Roy Tucker.

"I'd like to help out the club, Spike, only not at third base. Any other position, sure. But third, I couldn't risk it. I couldn't go through what I've been through the past year. Next season if you want, when my back is stronger and healed completely, when I've got my confidence again. Not this fall, Spike." All the time Roy was thinking of those sleepless nights, of the agony under the lamp in Florida, of the bars at the head of the bed twisted inward, of the operations and the pain and that gnawing toothache up and down his hip when he had tried to play baseball before he was ready.

No, he thought, not even for a pennant. I'll give it everything I've got, everything. I'll crash the fences and stand up there to the dusters and go round the bases with my spikes high. But not that. I won't take chances on this leg again; that's one thing I can't do. I won't risk going through what I've been through the past two years. That's out. I couldn't endure that pain. He doesn't understand, but that's how it is. I just couldn't.

All the while Spike was thinking, too. He's frightened. He's a different Roy Tucker. It's the first time I ever asked him that he didn't come across, the first time. I don't get it; I don't know what's biting him. Yet when a guy like that scares, there must be a reason for it. Some players, you tell 'em what to do or else. Not this bird. He isn't Lester Young.

It was a couple of weary ballclubs that came almost to the end of the journey that warm September afternoon at Ebbets Field. Both dressing rooms were tense spots as the boys got ready for battle. No need for meetings or fight talks. Everyone realized the pennant was at stake in that game, and these teams had met so often during the season and knew each other so well, talking was unnecessary. They knew each other's pitchers and batters, the pull hitters and the opposite field hitters; who was hard to throw to at the plate because he choked up on his bat; who had the arm to be feared in the field; who was so slow you could play back on the grass and nab him at first; and who was the guy to watch when loose on the sacks. Only one person was an unknown quantity. That was Steve Tracy, the new third baseman brought down by the Dodgers from Montreal. And the Cards were determined to find out about him before the afternoon was finished.

Inside the Dodger clubhouse that day, only Raz was his usual loquacious self. Notwithstanding the fact that he might have to take an important role that afternoon, he was unconcerned and voluble as ever. Not without purpose, for he was trying his best to amuse his teammates, to keep them from tightening up for the fray ahead.

[219]

"Stubblebeard—everyone hates that mean old fella. When I was with the Pirates before the war, Jake Smith gives it to Stubble plenty. He was always bearing down, making things tough for Jake. Now one day, Jake he's pitching to Bi Thomas of the Reds, hits him on the back and knocks him down. Bi has quite a temper, so he goes for Jake and they tangle. Well, Stubble's the plate ump, and o'course, he's got to put in his ten cents' worth. So he gets in there trying to separate 'em, and they all roll in the dirt together. Jake sees his chance. Well, be darned if the old chap doesn't come up with a black eye and a big lump behind his ear, though no one knows yet who give it to him. But he was damaged the worst of the three. Other ump, he comes along. 'What you doing down there, Stubble?' he asks. 'Me?' says the old man, rubbing that lump behind his ear. 'Oh, jest intervening.' "

They grinned feebly to please Raz; but they couldn't loosen up. Too much hung on it, far too much rode on every ball, hit or caught. Or not caught.

Outside there was a high sky. No sun shining, but high clouds, making it difficult for players to sight the ball. The Dodgers got to the Card southpaw for two runs in the first, when Roy, at his best in the clutch as usual, belted one down the foul line inside fair territory. Swanny and Lester scored to put the Brooks in the lead. Razzle, always poison for the Cards, held them in check. His fast ball was alive, his curve ball had sharper bends than a pretzel. He loved it, the capacity crowd, the shouts and cheers, the importance of the moment as he mowed the Redbirds down for the first three innings. He might indeed have completed the game in safety but for his infernal vanity.

With two down in the last of the third he managed by desperate racing to beat out an infield roller in a tight race for the bag with the first baseman, a sprint that left him gasping and puffing. Swanny promptly belted the ball on a clothesline to right, and Raz set forth. With a two-run lead there was no necessity to take any chances. The big hurler, however, fancied himself as a baserunner, and tore for third like a frightened fawn. Rounding second, he dashed for the scoring post, sliding into the bag through a hurricane of dust and dirt with all the grace of a water buffalo on the loose.

Smart baserunners seldom took any chances on Tommy Conlin's arm in right field, and a faster and less clumsy man on the sacks than Raz Nugent would have been nipped by the perfect throw that waited for him as he roared into third. Being the final out of the inning, he picked himself up, shook his head, dusted off his pants, and walked slowly across to the mound. Perhaps five minutes' rest, maybe only a couple of minutes sprawled out on the bench, would have given him back his wind and saved him. But he was tired from his exertion. The Cards knew it. This was their opportunity, and being smart ballplayers they immediately took it.

From his spot in center, Roy saw the whole drama. The first batter laid one down, a perfect dragged bunt on the grass equidistant from Razzle and the foul line. The pitcher lumbered across as young Tracy came charging in from third. Jocko called to Tracy to take it, but Raz half bent over and made a kind of stab at it. Then, seeing he couldn't reach the ball, he straightened up. They both stood watching it roll past.

That's bad, thought Roy. Oh, that's awful bad! That was young Tracy's ball; Raz shouldn't have tried to handle it. That wasn't the kid's fault, but it's bad. It will upset him right at this moment. And we better watch this man coming up now, we better watch him carefully; he's a mean man in a tight place.

All three outfielders shifted toward left field. Mickey Madden was a right hand batter, able to hit behind the runner, equally good at laying it down or pasting the ball past third. Roy noticed Razzle was trying hard to keep the ball so he couldn't bunt, but on the third pitch the big man lost control and came in low across the outside corner. Madden immediately put the wood to it and dragged the ball slowly down the third base line, a twisting, teasing roller, the hardest sort of a ball to handle.

The whole pattern of the field shifted before Roy's anxious gaze as he raced in toward second to back up a possible throw. He could see the runners digging in on the basepaths, and Raz's broad back, his legs wide apart on the mound, and young Tracy tearing in toward the ball. And above the noise and excitement, Jocko Klein's voice came to him:

"First . . . first . . . first . . ."

It was one of those plays where you do or you don't, where the fielder has to grab the ball with his bare hand and let go underhand without a moment's hesitation. Only a great third sacker could have handled it, and Steve Tracy was merely a rookie from Montreal thrown into the toughest kind of a baseball situation. Roy knew immediately that he would mess the play up, that he would fail to get the ball away cleanly. The boy snatched at it, reached for it, juggled it nervously. Actually he never even tried the throw at all.

The crowd roared, and the Redbirds hugged the sacks, and their coaches danced up and down behind first and third. The battle was on. Actually there were two battles that afternoon at Ebbets Field; the one between the Dodgers and the Cards that the fans all saw, and the one they didn't see— the battle Roy Tucker was fighting with himself. All his reason, his memory, his intelligence prevented him from taking over third base. But his instinct fought him every second. His instinct told him he was being a spectator when he should have been a competitor helping out his club in that hot spot in the infield.

Big Tommy Conlin lumbered up to the plate, an aggressive hitter facing a panting, worried man in the box. The batter took one, fouled off another, looked calmly at the third that was bad, and then teed off on the next pitch. It was a wicked liner, low

and at the third baseman's ankles, a bit to his right
so he had to reach. It was coming toward him, it
was at him, it was through. It was rolling and
bouncing and sizzling through the grass toward Paul
Roth in left field.

Roy raced across but Paul got there first, with a
perfect stop and a peg to third, a peg calculated
to hold the runner on the bag. But the rookie was
upset now and nervous. He was all thumbs, and the
ball got away from him. Just a few feet out on the
grass it rolled, out by the Cardinal coaching box,
and the dancing St. Louis coach, hands in the air.
Just a few feet it rolled, but enough. Like a shot the
baserunner was off and away for home.

On the bag stood the bewildered third baseman.
His head turned, now this way, now that, glancing
hastily around, searching for the ball.

"Behind you!"

"Behind!"

"Behind you!"

Spike yelled. Jocko shouted. Swanny shrieked
and Roy called out.

By the time Tracy recovered it, one run was over
and the other runner was on third, while the batter
was sliding desperately into second base. The Cards

were on the warpath again, fighting back, taking chances and coming through as they had done all summer long.

Roy could stand the agony no more. Instinct triumphed over intelligence. Slowly he walked through the tumult toward Spike Russell. Forgotten were the sleepless nights and the days of pain, the bent bars at the head of the bed, the suffering and the agony and the uncertainty whether he would ever play baseball again. Or even walk once more. All he could see was the diamond before his gaze, and the triumphant Redbirds on the sacks, and the one run over and the pennant going from their grasp.

So he came slowly into the infield, instinct conquering reason, the instinct of a competitor forcing him over to his manager at short. He said nothing, he merely reached out and put one hand on his skipper's arm as he went by. Then he stepped in at third, and Jocko, who understood, rolled the ball silently into the dirt at his feet. He scooped it up and laced it over to first.

"Tucker, No. 34, now playing third base for Brooklyn. Whitehouse, No. 6, in center field."

CHAPTER

27

THERE was a consultation around the box. Spike and Jocko and Raz and Roy stood together. Then a figure sauntered across from the bullpen, and once more the loudspeaker boomed out:

"Hathaway, No. 9, now pitching for Brooklyn."

The score was 2-1, there were runners on second and third, and no one down. A tough spot for a pitcher. But Bonesey was as cold as a landlord's heart. He took plenty of time, struck out the first batter, and got the second on a fly to Whitehouse, although the man from third scored to even things at 2-2. On the hit-and-run, the next batter dropped a lucky blooper into right which brought in another tally, and when the inning was over the Cards were leading, 3-2.

This was the score up to the end of the fifth. But

the Dodgers had been coming from behind all season; this was nothing new, just a bit harder because so much hung on it. They went to the woodpile with determination; they grasped their bats and stepped in to get that run back. Swanny racked it up, lining one down the right foul line, only great fielding holding him to a single. Feet wide apart, arms outstretched, he danced off the base while the stands erupted. As usual, their favorites were refusing to stay down for the count.

Lester, his batting eye back, promptly rifled a single through the hole between short and third. Pandemonium reigned as Roy jammed on the batter's cap and stepped to the plate. The crowd above rocked, roared, stamped, shrieked. They knew he wouldn't fail them. Two on, none out, an automatic warm-up situation. Out in right under the fence the Cardinal bullpen went furiously into action.

The first ball was wide. A shout rose, half anger, half delight. But the Redbirds were taking no chances. They weren't having any of Roy Tucker. There it goes, ball four! Roy slung away his bat, trotted to first, exchanging caps with Red Cassidy in the coaching box. The ballgame rode on a single pitch.

The canny lefthander in the box worked on Spike Russell, who was batting fourth, with everything he had: all his skill, all his control, all his brains. His side-arm curve made the batter step into the ball, made him reach out clumsily. Few hitters ever did much with Sam Chase's curves. But on the full count, Spike managed to lace an inside pitch on a line into the hole between center and right, going fast, not dropping, either. Vic Fleming, the great Cardinal speedster in center, came burning over like an express train, reached out, and speared the liner waist high with his gloved hand. His throw-in was at second before Lester could turn and back-track to safety. Then Roth popped up and the inning ended without any score.

As the game continued, Bones had the Cards throttled. Even on three balls and no strikes, with Jack MacManus above in a positive fury, Bonesey would come over the plate, full of assurance he would not be hit hard. He wasn't, either. He slid them across and curved them in and blazed them through, the Redbirds completely helpless before him. Every inning they went quickly out; every inning the Dodgers threatened and were unable to score that important run. Good fielding cut them down on the basepaths or robbed them of hits in the field. They came into the eighth, still a run behind, with the crowd pleading and yammering for that tally to save the situation.

Chase was weary and panting. It was almost the end of the game at the end of a long and exhausting season. Yet he appeared to be losing none of his stuff, to be getting stronger as the game went along. He had to be beaten; he refused to quit. In the Dodger dugout, the boys were grim. They chewed mechanically, they yanked at their caps; for once even Razzle, sitting on the bench in his jacket, was silent. They stood crowding the steps as Roy came to the slab. This was the big moment, the time for a rally if one was ever to come.

The Redbird pitcher was smart. Taking no chances on the Brooks' slugger at that critical moment, he gave Roy nothing to hit. He fouled off ball after ball; for five minutes the unending duel between smart hurler and canny hitter went on. Until on the 2 and 2 pitch, Roy swung. However, he only got a piece of the ball, which was exactly what Chase intended. It struck the plate and bounded high into the air, a Baltimore chop that did not come down in time to nail Roy at first. It was scratchy, but it was the start of a rally.

Spike followed with a smart bingle behind Roy into right field, but the Kid, in awe of that strong arm, stayed firmly anchored at second base. Now the Redbird bullpen was a fever of activity. The stands were seething as Paul Roth stepped in. Chase got ahead of him with two strikes and a ball, and then came in with a change of pace that was a beauty, sending Roth down swinging. A groan echoed over the stands. One out, and Bobby Russell at bat.

One run behind, one run needed. A clean single would do it, would push the winning run around to third and would bring the speedy Tucker home with the tieing counter. That was all they needed, a well-timed blow deep to the outfield. But Bob had orders. He bunted the third pitch cleanly down the first base line. There was a rush, a roar, and a stampede for the bag. Old Stubble hovered over the play, his arms extended, hands down as the lightning-fast Bobby flashed across the sack.

Instantly Stubble was surrounded by Cards. Don Lee, their first sacker, turned on him in a frenzy. He whanged the ball to the ground in disgust. It was enough for Roy. Without hesitation, he rounded third, hit the inside corner and struck out for the plate.

Lee, with his teammates shrieking in his ears, reached for the ball and hurled it at the catcher. The umpire was there, bending over, his mask in his hand, while Roy with one arm in the air slid across the platter to score the tieing run.

The Cards protested. They claimed Bob Russell was out at first. They insisted they had called time. They yelled and yowled. Chase was the loudest of all; he declared they were being robbed by the Brooklyn umpires. He closed in on old Stubblebeard. The ancient umpire stood undisturbed, his arms folded, listening, while the Brooks watched with exuberance from the bench.

"That old Stubblebeard now, he ain't such a bad fella; knows his stuff, he really does; he won't take any nonsense from those Redbirds." "See there! Looka there!" "Yes, sir, there he goes, there he goes!" "There goes Chase! And more of 'em, too, if they don't pipe down pretty quick."

The unfortunate Chase was being sent from the field. When the confusion died away and the new pitcher entered the game, Spike was perched on third and the score was tied at 3-3. The manager came home a minute later on Jocko Klein's timely lift to deep right center, and by the end of the inning the Dodgers were once again in the lead by that all-important run. On the scoreboard in right went the blessed, the wonderful figure 2.

Three outs to get. Three more outs and the game is ours. And the pennant too, for if we win this one they'll never catch us.

CHAPTER

28

THE nervous ninth, with every man, every woman, and every kid in the ballpark on their feet, tense with emotion. The nervous ninth, and the last three outs to get, the toughest in any ballgame. And the crowd ready to tear the place apart brick by brick.

Then it happened. It wasn't Bonesey's fault, or anyone's. Actually it was one of those breaks that come to a team in a game, bad only when they come at an important moment. Don Lee, the husky Card first sacker, smacked a sizzling grounder that Spike could easily have handled. It struck Bonesey's foot and rose high in the air. Roy, charging across, snared it falling and pegged it on a line to first. The throw was good but it reached the base just as the runner flashed past. A man on first and no one out. The nervous ninth indeed.

Now the Brooklyn bullpen went into action; Jerry and old Fat Stuff and Mike Mehaffey began to pour it in to their catchers. Out on the mound, Bonesey visited the rosin bag before starting to throw to Tony Carone, the St. Louis left fielder.

This was the time, this was the moment. The signal was passed round and acknowledged by all the men concerned. Suddenly Roy realized that in his new spot he was at the nerve center of a ball-club. He liked it. He liked being in the heart of things; he was a clutch player and he reveled in the excitement, and the danger, too. It aroused his competitive instinct. He forgot his injury, forgot the long illness behind him. And he felt how close they were together, how vital every man was on every play.

With Lee on first and Carone at bat, Bonesey followed the signs and threw wide on the second pitch. Both Roy and Lester Young, who had been hugging the bag, dashed half way toward the plate as if to cover a bunt. Lee at once took a wide lead off first. He was unprepared for Bob Russell's light-ning dash behind him to first base. Vainly the St. Louis coach shrieked and yelled. Jocko's peg to

[235]

Bob was perfect, low to the outside, and Bob put the ball on the runner, nailing him cold.

Now the Brooklyn stands had a chance to yell. One out and no one aboard and the Dodgers still leading by a run. The Card left fielder stepped back into the batter's box. He waited calmly for the 2 and 1 pitch, and then belted a clothesline into center field.

It was a race and a close one out in the garden. Al Whitehouse charged it, digging like mad to collar that ball on the first hop and cut the speedy runner off at third base. He grabbed the ball on the bounce and threw to Roy over third. But the Cards needed that run badly, and their coach held Carone at second, taking no chances at this critical moment of the game. One on, and one down.

Then what they had all been expecting followed. It was precisely the same play which Steve Tracy had messed up earlier in the game: a slow, dragged bunt along the baseline half way to third.

Roy hesitated. He was on his toes, yet he hesitated in starting. Fear, or something stronger, that instinctive desire to protect his weakness which was now almost habit, kept him from making a sudden forward leap. Held in place a fraction of a second, he was slow off the mark. Once away his movements were fast. Racing in, he stabbed the ball with his bare hand, whirled, and forced the runner on second back.

Now the long throw to first, the race between the Cardinal runner and the ball, the field umpire running over toward the bag watching, and then the roar as the Redbird swept across the hassock just as the throw reached Lester's outstretched mitt.

They stood there tossing the ball about the infield, exchanging it with quick, nervous gestures. Roy handled it last and, rubbing it up, walked slowly toward the box. He knew what Bonesey was thinking and indeed what they were all thinking. That I'm scared; that I can't take it; that I'm not the old Roy Tucker.

He knew his slip-up would react upon them, for they were a team and so closely united that what happened to one had an effect on the rest. Especially on the younger and sensitive ones like their temperamental pitcher. Some of the old-timers, Fat Stuff, for instance, forgot a bumble in the field as soon as it happened. But Bonesey always felt those things in a critical moment of a game. And when someone

[237]

made a spectacular catch or came up with a double-play ball, he would bear down harder than ever.

Roy walked slowly back to his position. Shoot, I should have had that one. It wasn't too hard a chance. I should have had it; I would have had it, too, if only I'd got away as I used to do. Two men aboard and only one out. We ought to have two down and the game in our pocket. That's bad. It'll hurt Bonesey, this will.

It did, too. Bonesey, who was tiring, suddenly lost control and couldn't find the plate.

One ball. Yes, sir, there he goes! Two balls. He's finished now. Wide, three balls. No mistake, he's through. Then the batter was slinging away his bat and trotting down toward first. Three men on the sacks, and my fault, all my fault, too.

The Cardinal dugout, with every man on the step, was delirious. In the coaching boxes the two St. Louis veterans were dancing with delight. For any kind of a long ball, a lazy single to the outfield, meant a couple of runs, and even a fly ball would tie the score. To them the game was as good as won. All around the ballpark the crowd was up shouting, while Spike turned toward the bullpen in left, and Roy, his head down, walked across to his position on the grass by third.

Yep, there goes Bonesey—he's done. And all my fault. He'd never have lost control if I'd nabbed that man on first. A pitcher's only as good as his support. I quit on the boys, and there goes old Bonesey.

Actually Spike, signaling to the bullpen, had little choice. Jerry Fielding, his fastest and most dependable hurler, was needed for the next afternoon. So, rather than string along with some youngster on his staff, he picked a veteran. To call in old Fat Stuff was taking a chance. But Spike Russell was a chance-taker and knew when to take them.

One down, the bases loaded, one run ahead in the ninth, and the milling thousands in the stands pleading for a stopper to the Cardinal rally. That was the situation they handed the veteran from the bullpen. He came hurrying across, half-waddling on his short, thick legs, over to where Spike was rolling the ball nervously in his glove. Jocko, with the tools on, was waiting for him on the mound. Swinging up to the plate was Stevie Richards, a .300 hitter, one of the best in the business and a man who had knocked in ninety runs that season.

Fat Stuff merely laid one hand on his skipper's shoulder. "Gimme that ball."

Then he stepped into the box and slapped his young catcher on the back. Jocko walked to the plate and the veteran with a quick movement and little wind-up threw in a few warm-up pitches. He looked at the runners on the sacks. He nodded to Spike. He was set to go.

His first ball to the batter was across the letters and drew a loud foul to the screen. Then two wasted ones, the pitcher driving the Cardinal slugger away from the slab with low, inside pitches. Next a change of pace that caught the edge of the plate for strike two; then a high one off the point of the chin that the batter took for the third ball and the full count.

Through it all, Fat Stuff was unhurried and un-worried. In the midst of that bedlam he stood on the mound, his chin out, glancing coolly around the sacks as he checked the three runners, completely master of the situation. The three Redbirds danced back and forth with outstretched arms upon the basepaths. From the coaching boxes the two coaches shouted defiance through cupped hands. At the plate the batter stood deep, waiting for one to hit.

He never got it. Instead, Fat Stuff sneaked in a fast ball over the corner and Richards swung round vainly in an attempt to crack it. Two out and still three men aboard. Still anyone's game.

But now it was the Brooklyn turn to yell and yell they did: the Knot Hole Gang in deep center; the kids who lined up early in the morning to get a spot in the bleachers; the folks in the two-dollar seats and the people in the boxes down front; and the fans in the upper tiers reaching almost around the field. They stood cheering the old man's effort, while the shadows deepened over the field and the September sun sank lower and lower in the sky.

Roy picked up some dirt and tossed it away as Mike Madden stepped forward, rubbing rosin on his hands, hitching his belt before stepping into the batter's box. What's the matter with me, Roy thought. I'm afraid. I don't *think* I'm afraid; yet it holds me back in the clutches. I'm afraid. And of what?

Suddenly there came to him words he had heard as a youngster, words he had heard men repeat many times before, words he had often read but that had had no real meaning to him. For the first time now they had a meaning. "The only thing we have to fear is fear itself." Forget this thing that's

[241]

holding me back. Forget it. The only thing to fear is fear.

Big Mike, swinging that war-club, stood leaning forward, watching Fat Stuff, motionless as a statue in the box. The old man nodded to Jocko, took a last look round the bags, gave his short, quick wind-up and let go. Mike hit. Up in the air.

This time Roy was off as the ball was struck. No delay, no hesitation; with a bound he sprang to his right and was off.

It was high to the side, it was a wide foul, beyond his reach. Paul Roth and Jocko and Spike realized this instantly as the ball rose in the air and began to descend.

"Can't get it!"

"Foul, Roy, foul!"

But he was giving it nothing. Straining desperately, he went in closer, nearing the low boxes back of third. Forgetting everything but the twisting falling ball above, he rushed headlong toward the stands, closer now, closer.

"*Watch it, Roy, watch it!*"

"*Watch it . . . look out!*"

He couldn't look out. He couldn't slow up. He could only sight that falling ball, dropping there just beyond his grasp. A step, a few steps, and it was there, almost within his reach.

Then the low rail of the front boxes smashed into his thigh with a terrific blow. Off balance he lunged, jumped forward with a last-second stab, and speared the ball with his gloved hand as he plunged over the rail and into the box. His shoulder whanged against an iron chair hastily vacated by a frightened customer. His head hit something hard as he tumbled to the concrete floor. His shoulders first, then his body, and then his legs disappeared from sight. But the ball was in his mitt.

Someone helped him up, yanked him to his feet, and pulled him out onto the field again. He tossed the ball to the grass and staggered ahead until someone put an arm about his shoulder and led him toward the dugout. His hip ached where he had fallen, his arm was skinned where he had scraped it on the floor, his head hurt where he had smacked it. But he had held that ball. The game was over.

Now it was hard to reach the bench through that tornado of fans and players and kids swarming around, that crazy mob which tried to sweep him from his feet. The Dodgers swung in about Roy, pounding his lame back, half-carrying him into the dugout, and so down the long passageway under the stands, separated from that crowd only by a wire grill. They were yelling, the team was, joyous and exultant and happy and half dead, all at the same time.

"Twelve years in the big time, and I never saw anything like it," remarked Fat Stuff to everyone and to no one in particular in the press surging by. He wiped his face with the sleeve of his sweat shirt. "No, sir, I never saw anything to touch it. Or that-there kid, either." He found himself walking along beside the ubiquitous Casey. "Casey, six months ago he couldn't even walk. Why, I saw him on a bed in the hotel, and he wasn't able to hobble across the room. I'm tellin' ya, six months ago the kid couldn't even walk!"

They stomped into the clubhouse, setting up a din you could hear outside. Tomorrow was another day. They had won the opener, they had the Cards' number. The photographers thought so too, for they surrounded the team, Spike and Roy and Bonesey and Fat Stuff and the rest. The manager had to pose with the old man, with his arm around Roy, then around Bonesey, then with his brother.

When the reporters tried to talk to the young

skipper, they had to drag him by main force away from the cameramen who were around him, as usual pleading for "Just one more, Spike, just one more, please. Look this way . . . here . . . over here . . . this way, Spike."

Finally the newspapermen pinned him in his room. He sat on a chair stripped to his pants, far too excited to collect his thoughts as they peppered him with questions.

Someone turned to Fat Stuff, sitting beside his manager, still in his soaking clothes. "What was the best thing you had out there this afternoon, old-timer?"

The veteran threw up his hands. "You guys and your questions! The best thing I had out there today was my fielders." He pointed over to the main room where a boy sitting on a chair was peeled down to the buff. There was an enormous patch of red skin where he had attempted to break down the rail on a third base box. And the trainer was working intently over an angry-looking shoulder, trying to get it in shape for the next afternoon.

Fat Stuff pointed at him. "The best thing I had out there today was my fielders, and especially that-there Kid from Tomkinsville."